D0640929

# THE CHRISTMAS APPEAL

Also from Janice Hallett and Atria Books

*The Appeal*

*The Twyford Code*

*The Mysterious Case of the Alperton Angels*

*The Examiner* (2024)

# THE CHRISTMAS APPEAL

### A Novella

# *Janice Hallett*

**ATRIA** BOOKS

New York • London • Toronto • Sydney • New Delhi

**ATRIA**
BOOKS

An Imprint of Simon & Schuster, Inc.
1230 Avenue of the Americas
New York, NY 10020

First Atria Books hardcover edition October 2023

**ATRIA** BOOKS and colophon are trademarks of Simon & Schuster, Inc.

Simon & Schuster: Celebrating 100 Years of Publishing Since 1924

For information about special discounts for bulk purchases, please contact Simon & Schuster Special Sales at 1-866-506-1949 or business@simonandschuster.com.

The Simon & Schuster Speakers Bureau can bring authors to your live event. For more information or to book an event, contact the Simon & Schuster Speakers Bureau at 1-866-248-3049 or visit our website at www.simonspeakers.com.

Manufactured in the United States of America

1 3 5 7 9 10 8 6 4 2

Library of Congress Cataloging-in-Publication Data has been applied for.

ISBN 978-1-6680-3588-7
ISBN 978-1-6680-3589-4 (ebook)

*For the Ghost of Christmas Past*

These are but shadows of the things that have been.

—*A Christmas Carol* by Charles Dickens, 1843

# THE CHRISTMAS APPEAL

To: Femi Hassan & Charlotte Holroyd
From: Roderick Tanner, KC
Date: November 1, 2023
Subject: A conundrum for you

Dear both,

I trust you are well.

While you establish yourselves in the field of criminal law, it doesn't hurt to keep the wheels of deduction turning. I have another fascinating case to run past you. Why you? Well, it seems The Fairway Players are once again at the center of a mystery.

I've read the enclosed and think I've worked it out. I wonder if *you* can.

Here is a bundle of correspondence from the last few weeks of 2022, during rehearsals for the pantomime *Jack and the Beanstalk*.

I look forward to hearing your thoughts.

RT
Roderick Tanner, KC (retired)

**Charlotte**
Warning! Incoming trigger alert.

**Femi**
Yes. I've just opened the six-megabyte attachment.

**Charlotte**
Seems he's not enjoying his retirement as much as he thought.

**Femi**
I'm not enjoying his retirement as much as I thought.

**Charlotte**
I've scrolled through the doc. It's a bundle of e-discovery scans. They *do* look intriguing.

**Femi**
Given how he's helped us in the past, we can't very well say no.

To: [Address List]
From: Celia Halliday
Date: December 1, 2022
Subject: A wonderful year!

Dear all,

Kerplunk! Another year of living, loving, and laughing.

You'll excuse the round-robin email. We no longer send Christmas cards as they are so bad for the environment. More than that, we have such a vast number of friends that writing to you all individually would take far too long—so we only send personal emails to family and those we are especially close to.

Now if you're anything like us, then you faced every challenge that came your way in 2022, picked it up, gave it a wink, and firmly knocked it out of the park. Here is a full and fabulous account of our wonderful year.

Firstly, our skiing vacation in Val d'Isère was almost cut short when Joel had some life-changing news . . . ta-da! He was made OBE for his charity work! What a wonderful surprise and validation of his selfless sacrifice over the years. The award of Officer of the Most Excellent Order of the British Empire comes with onerous responsibility. He had to change his credit, debit, library, gym, National Trust, and Waitrose loyalty cards to feature the three little letters he is legally required to place after his name.

Spring saw the first production this year by The Fairway Players. Current chair Sarah-Jane MacDonald, who insisted on retaining her post despite giving birth to baby Sammy last year, chose the so-called "comedy" *An Evening with Gary Lineker* by Arthur Smith and Chris England. Kevin MacDonald directed and Sarah-Jane produced. Despite a few last-minute cast changes that saw the part of Gary Lineker played by sixty-seven-year-old Joyce Walford, the play was surprisingly watchable.

Our gorgeous, beautiful, and talented daughter, Beth, celebrated her twentieth birthday in June. She took a break from her studies at Oxford University and came home, thinking we would celebrate with a quiet family dinner—little did she know we'd organized a surprise party at the exclusive, members-only River Club in Lockley Bois, where rumor has it Joanna Lumley once dined. Beth's good friends Frankie Bridge and Rochelle Humes, from chart-topping girl band The Saturdays, put their solo careers on hold to attend and treated us all to an impromptu a cappella version of "What About Us."

Autumn saw Joel and Celia finally get their chance to direct and produce a Fairway play, *Glengarry Glen Ross* by David Mamet. It was a controversial choice, but as everyone knows, the Hallidays are always at the front of the line when challenges are handed out. This is a stage classic that won the Pulitzer Prize in 1984, no less! Of course that was a long time ago and we felt the original script would benefit from a few tweaks, so we removed the swearing, changed the setting to Lockwood so that we could use our own accents, and gave it a happy ending. David Mamet himself sent his congratulations on a triumphant production.

Our son Gregory's property business won the contract to sell all the luxury new-builds on the area now known as Hayward Heights. The largest properties were featured in *Country Life* and appeared as "must sees" in the property section of *The Sunday Times*. He was also a consultant for the council when they built the Grange Estate, a mix of housing-association accommodation and help-to-buy starter homes on the *other* side of Lockwood. He celebrated with a boys' vacation (look out, girls!) to Mykonos and Santorini—the two most expensive islands in the Mediterranean.

Even Woof has had a successful year! Our beautiful rescue dog, which we so generously gave a home to, was awarded "Mutt with the Most" at the spring fair.

Has this letter reached the bottom of the page already? But we haven't even mentioned Celia's prizewinning crocheted fruit, Beth's vacation in Portugal in a luxury villa with its own butler, Joel's new car—a vintage Aston Martin—and Gregory's advanced driving course, open only to carefully selected drivers.

Phew! So before we wish you all a very merry Christmas and a happy New Year, we would just like to say: as a family, we smash through any obstacle in our path and treat every moment as if it were our last. We are prouder of both our children with each passing day.

Merry Christmas and Happy New Year!
Celia and Joel Halliday, OBE

---

To: Celia Halliday
From: Jackie Marsh
Date: December 1, 2022
Subject: [automatic out of office reply] Re: A wonderful year!

On vacation, Jackie

I USED TO COUNT EVERY PENNY NOW I COUNT MY CRYPTOCOIN MILLIONS YOU CAN DO THE SAME! CALL TOLL-FREE ON 0800-0300-000 AND WATCH YOUR WEALTH GROOOOOO

To: Celia Halliday
From: Joyce Walford
Date: December 1, 2022
Subject: Re: A wonderful year!

Christmas comes around earlier every year. It'll be in August next.

January they put a trash can near Harry's grave before he was even cold in it. Now it overflows onto his stone. February my neighbor had a biopsy, but it turned out benign. March nothing happened. April I was Gary Lineker and I've never liked him. Barry came off his bike in May, but he was all right. June and July are far too hot these days. August they put a dropped curb in front of next door—now Nick can't park his work van there. September to now, nothing happened. A normal year really.

What about your Peter, Celia? Is he out yet? Joyce

---

To: Sarah-Jane MacDonald
From: Carol Dearing
Date: December 1, 2022
Subject: Bloody Celia!

Bloody Celia Halliday has sent out her Christmas round-robin! It's December the first, for goodness' sake! And what she said about *An Evening with Gary Lineker*—I could throttle her. You and Kevin did a wonderful job with that play. No one noticed it was Joyce in the England kit. "Surprisingly watchable," my bottom! It was a resounding success.

I feel like replying with more accurate footnotes:

- She doesn't send Christmas cards because she's as tight as a gnat's you-know-what.
- Joel was awarded an OBE because his brother-in-law is on the honors committee.
- "Three little letters he is legally required to place after his name"? Balls! Unless it stands for Overcome By Egocentricity.
- Beth has dropped out of university, which incidentally is Oxford Brookes (NOT the centuries-old institution Celia deliberately misleads everyone into thinking it is).
- Beth is not "friends" with The Saturdays—they were paid to attend the party and were contracted to sing one song.
- David Mamet sent not his congratulations, but a lawyer's letter threatening legal action for breach of copyright.
- The advanced driving course is a speed-awareness scheme. Gregory (who is openly gay) was caught, along with every other resident of Lockwood, exceeding the new 20 mph limit past the big Tesco.
- "We are prouder of both our children with each passing day"? What of middle son, Peter? His exploits haven't made the Christmas round-robin since 2013 when he won a half marathon—which turned out to be at a youth detention center, otherwise described by his parents as an "exclusive activity camp."
- And Woof is the mutt with the "most" revolting habits. I swear she brings him to Fairways deliberately to disrupt you. That dog didn't come to a single *Glengarry* rehearsal—not one!

Rant over. How is my lovely little big boy Harley and baby Samantha? I can't wait to have them both over on Sunday. I'll look after Sammy while you're rehearsing. We can't have the Hallidays claiming the "most triumphant production of the year" when it's going to be your panto. If you ask me, they've never got over you and Kevin being voted joint chair of The Fairways committee. She's that competitive.

Is *your* Christmas email ready to go? You don't want to look disorganized. Mum

---

To: Carol Dearing
From: Sarah-Jane MacDonald
Date: December 1, 2022
Subject: Re: Bloody Celia!

No, Mum, it's not, and you deserve a medal for reading to the end. It lost me at "kerplunk." Celia and Joel are sulking because the committee has vetoed their next choice of play. They wanted to do *When Did You Last See Your Trousers?* A *farce*, for heaven's sake! Everyone knows farce is dead. Ignore them and they'll soon get over it.

Harley is studying for his history test and Sammy is asleep at long last. Can I bring her over at five instead of six? I need to sweet-talk the vicar into removing a stud wall behind the stage to make room for the beanstalk. It's enormous, is over forty years old, and has been in countless pantos, but it's by far the best beanstalk in the local area. We need a good, sturdy stem for Jack to climb up. When you can clearly see that a group has cobbled a beanstalk together and Jack mimes climbing it, well, the story loses all credibility for me.

I've tracked it down to Fowey Light Operatic Society. Their chair, Jock, is storing it in his lockup. Mick Payne offered to collect it in his van. The Walford boys will help carry it. Kevin and Joel will meet them here and they'll all maneuver the beanstalk through the church hall and onto the stage. We just need the vicar's permission to take the wall down for the duration of rehearsals and performance nights. Wish me luck.

---

To: The Fairway Players' Committee
From: Kevin MacDonald
Date: December 1, 2022
Subject: Draft Program

Ok, folks, here's draft text for the program. Remember, this is a one-night-only fundraising evening. The program is a single sheet of paper, folded in two, that I print off at work, so no requests for color photographs or gold-embossed lettering. Any mistakes or typos, let me know before the ninth—or four ever holed you're piece. Kevin

The Fairway Players present
# Jack and the Beanstalk

First performed at The London Palladium in 1978
All proceeds in aid of the Church Hall Roof

Cast
(In order of appearance)

| | |
|---|---|
| Jack Trott | *Emma Crooks* |
| Dame Trott | *Joel Halliday* |
| "Simple" Simon Trott | *Harley MacDonald* |
| Callous Hands the Wage Snatcher | *John O'Dea* |
| Mr. Ugly the Village Idiot | *Matthew Dexter* |
| Daisy the Cow | *Nick and Barry Walford* |
| Fairy Godmother | *Beth Halliday* |
| Mr. Bean Dealer | *Mick Payne* |
| Buxom Betty | *Carly Dexter* |
| Princess Jill of Cloud Land | *Fran Elroy-Jones* |
| King of Cloud Land | *Mick Payne* |
| Queen of Cloud Land | *Celia Halliday* |
| The Giant's voice | *Kevin MacDonald* |

Nonspeaking villagers and fairies, etc.
Karen Payne, Marianne Payne, Denise Malcolm, Joyce Walford,
Dustin Perez, Myra Briggs

| | |
|---|---|
| Director | Sarah-Jane MacDonald |
| Producer | Kevin MacDonald |
| Music | Harley MacDonald |
| Costumes and makeup | Marianne Payne, Denise Malcolm |
| Refreshments | Joyce Walford |
| Set building and stage management | Joel Halliday |

### Join The Fairway Players

If you picture yourself sweeping down a golden staircase, sweeping an adoring audience off its feet, or just plain sweeping up, The Fairway Players needs YOU. We are a well-established, friendly group committed to delivering quality entertainment to the local community. We stage two theatrical productions a year, as well as our annual pantomime, in this church hall, and we're always keen to welcome new members. Contact Celia Halliday for details.

### Now & Zen
Yoga with Emma
Bend, stretch, breathe,
let it go

### John O'Dea
Retired accountant
Help with tax, VAT, etc.
Motto: "It all adds up"

**Message posted to The Fairway Players' Committee's WhatsApp group on December 1, 2022:**

**Celia**

May I remind everyone on the committee, and especially those responsible for printed material issued on behalf of the group, that Joel's name should *always* be followed by the letters OBE, whenever and wherever it appears. Tiresome, I know, but it's a legal requirement and the law is clear.

---

**Message exchange between Sarah-Jane and Kevin MacDonald on December 1, 2022:**

2:11 p.m. Sarah-Jane wrote:
We had this with Glengarry and Gary Lineker. Do you deliberately "forget" Joel's OBE every time you send draft program text? Are you really that petty?

2:15 p.m. Kevin wrote:
You bet I do. And yes, I am.

2:21 p.m. Sarah-Jane wrote:
Remember, we must stand for reelection as joint chairs every year, and exhibitions of pique will only fuel the Hallidays' next campaign. I like to think we are cochairs through our hard work, clear heads, and sense of fairness. To lead, we must put away childish things.

2:26 p.m. Kevin wrote:
Well said. Joel, OBE will be described as Joel, OBE whenever Joel, OBE is mentioned. Signed, Kevin, no-BE.

To: Celia Halliday
From: Fran Elroy-Jones
Date: December 2, 2022
Subject: Music

Dear Celia,

I overheard you speaking to someone at the last rehearsal about how disappointing it is that we don't have live music for the pantomime, purely because no current members are musical or know anyone who is.

I'm new and don't know how things work, but I used to play sax at university and am still in touch with a few musicians. I could ask around. There may be someone who wants performance experience, and you only need a keyboard player, drummer, and guitarist. Sarah-Jane is always so busy, I thought I'd ask you if it's worth me putting forward the suggestion, or perhaps you could mention it for me? Thank you, Fran

---

To: Fran Elroy-Jones
From: Celia Halliday
Date: December 2, 2022
Subject: Re: Music

Dear Fran,

First, may I say what a wonderful princess you make. Someone with as beautiful a singing voice as you have deserves proper accompaniment and, agreed, a live trio of musicians would make for a much better production.

However, on balance, we feel it's far better for Sarah-Jane to forge ahead with her creative vision for *Jack and the Beanstalk*, even though it means the actors sing along to tracks played on Spotify by her surly teenage son. She's even chosen an opening number because it mentions "a room without a roof," as if our audience will link that to the church hall roof! There are no literary scholars in Lockwood.

We have no doubt that the shortcomings of that decision will be glaringly obvious to all on the night. When everyone finally realizes her limitations, it will make for a less busy Sarah-Jane all around. My best advice to you, Fran, is to keep quiet and let nature take its course.

On another note, how are you settling in on Hayward Heights? Our son Gregory was the handsome dish who sold you the house. At first we wondered how someone who worked at a supermarket with Karen Payne could ever afford to live there, but then we found out you're the Regional Manager and it all made sense. If you ever fancy meeting up with Greg for a drink or a chat about property, it can be arranged! Best, Celia

---

To: Celia Halliday
From: Dustin Perez
Date: December 2, 2022
Subject: Recruitment drive

Dear Celia,
Sarah-Jane said at the last rehearsal we need new members to increase the volume of our crowd scenes and to let you know any ideas, as you're membership secretary. I'm new to Fairways and wonder if you'd like me to distribute leaflets on the Grange Estate? Like everyone else there, I've just moved in and I'm sure many will

be looking for local activities to join. I'm enjoying rehearsals so much, I'm more than happy to let others know about the group. Dustin

---

To: Dustin Perez
From: Celia Halliday
Date: December 2, 2022
Subject: Re: Recruitment drive

The Grange Estate is on the *other* side of the big Tesco, and most people there don't have cars or much interest in theater. Celia

---

To: Sarah-Jane MacDonald
From: Rev. Joshua Harries
Date: December 2, 2022
Subject: Money

Dear Mrs. MacDonald,

Thank you so much for popping in to see me this evening and for the news that all profits from *Jack and the Beanstalk* will be donated to our roof fund. The Fairway Players are welcome to remove the partition backstage to make way for the beanstalk. I would ask, though, that you take great care of the wall panel, as the church committee simply can't afford to replace it. May I suggest you store it in the greenroom?

Do break a leg for the performance, and may the booing and hissing be in all the right places! Yours, Rev. Harries

---

**Message exchange between Sarah-Jane and Kevin MacDonald on December 2, 2022:**

6:41 p.m. Kevin wrote:
Christ in Crocs! This beanstalk must be made of lead.

6:42 p.m. Sarah-Jane wrote:
It's a PROFESSIONAL beanstalk.

6:45 p.m. Kevin wrote:
Jock says it's so cumbersome most local groups don't bother with it these days. It's been in his lockup since 2016. Smells like a butcher's rag.

6:46 p.m. Kevin wrote:
The beanstalk, not Jock. He smells of Lynx Africa.

6:47 p.m. Sarah-Jane wrote:
Where is it now? It MUST be safely secured in place before tomorrow's rehearsal.

6:52 p.m. Kevin wrote:
We're taking a breather at the entrance to the hall. It's leaning precariously against the storm porch—pic attached.

6:54 p.m. Sarah-Jane wrote:
BE CAREFUL! Other drama groups will want to use it again when they see how impressive it is. Is that a split in the trunk?

6:56 p.m. Kevin wrote:
Yes, you can just see the polystyrene filler inside. Nick said he'll gaffer-tape it and do any repairs later.

6:57 p.m. Sarah-Jane wrote:

Good. How are Mick, Nick, and Barry doing?

6:58 p.m. Kevin wrote:

Mick's cholesterol is 6.6, Nick's van is playing up, and Barry's besotted with his new girlfriend.

6:58 p.m. Sarah-Jane wrote:

I mean, are they pulling their weight? Please assure them all their hard work will be worth it. This beanstalk will make our panto stand out. I promise.

---

To: The Fairway Players' mailing list
From: Sarah-Jane MacDonald
Date: December 3, 2022
Subject: Jack and the Beanstalk

Dear Fairway Players,

Surely The Fairway Players' annual panto can't be less than three weeks away? Oh, yes it is!

For any new members who might not be aware, we spend the month of December frantically rehearsing a fundraising pantomime that we perform for one night only, just before the big day. In fact, some of us consider the *panto* to be the big day, and Christmas merely an after-party. The funds we raise this year will benefit the church hall roof, a cause familiar to anyone involved in *An Evening with Gary Lineker* earlier this year, when a chain of events I won't go into here led to the postponement of the show.

Despite a short rehearsal time and a single performance, the panto generates almost as much admin, and therefore stress, as our regular productions, so it's all-hands-on-deck for set building, costume making, and ticket sales. We have fewer active members these days, so more tasks for the committee, but hopefully this will not be for long! Leaflets for *Jack and the Beanstalk* include full membership details. Given that two new housing developments have been built in and around Lockwood over the last couple of years, this production is the perfect opportunity to "fish" for new members and swell our ranks once again. Please spread the word whenever and wherever you can.

I'm delighted to say we've procured a real beanstalk! Huge thanks to Kevin, Mick, Barry, and Nick who collected it from Fowey Light Op. Soc. and managed to hoist it onstage without any lasting injury. It's now firmly in position and looks spectacular. Nine feet wide at the base and eighteen feet tall, it bends at the top, so the audience won't notice that it's technically a bit too big for our performance space. This means that Emma—in her role as principal boy, Jack—can climb the beanstalk for real and disappear at the top as if she's actually being swallowed by the clouds. I can't tell you how exciting this is. Those of us who saw the Mendham Players stage the same production last year will remember they wrapped green tinsel around a stepladder and you could clearly see their Jack step off it onto a stack of pallets.

This beanstalk is particularly special. It began life on the West End stage many years ago—so just imagine the stars who will have acted alongside it. However, it's not getting any younger and, close-up, I notice it is a little scuffed and dirty, thanks to the Fowey's damp lockup, so any volunteers willing to wield a cloth and paintbrush would be very much appreciated.

We've had to store a wall panel backstage in the greenroom, so I'm afraid we'll be rather cramped for this production. It's not ideal, but it'll be worth the inconvenience when we all gather around the foot of the stalk, look up, and see Emma ascending to a magical land.

All that remains for me to say is that we have only eight rehearsals left before we perform *Jack and the Beanstalk* in front of a live audience on Friday, December 23. So, please, if you can help the production before, during, or after the big night, do let me know.

Sarah-Jane MacDonald
Cochair of The Fairway Players

---

To: The Fairway Players' mailing list
From: Celia Halliday
Date: December 3, 2022
Subject: Jack and the Beanstalk

Dear Fairway Players,
Fee Fie Foe Fur—I smell the blood of a Fairway Play-er!

Seriously, the pantomime is The Fairway Players' annual opportunity to connect with the local community through their children and raise much-needed funds that allow us to stage top-notch productions throughout the year.

The audience expects—indeed, *wants*—rough-and-ready entertainment with a relaxed approach to costumes and scenery. After all, it takes more imagination and is much more fun to slap paint on a few pieces of cardboard than buy ready-made props used to death by other groups. The children don't notice, and the adults find it funny—win-win!

Nonetheless, Joel would like to see as many members as possible at set building on Sunday. The sharp-witted among you will have picked up on the fact we have *less* time to paint and plaster, but *more* scenery to prepare, all of which must now be redesigned around a monolithic beanstalk. There's Jack's cottage, the road to market, Cloud Village, and the Giant's castle. It's lucky for us that, in Joel Halliday, OBE, we have the best, most creative set designer and builder the group has ever known.

Accruing new members is all very well—if those members are young, fit, and talented, with a positive attitude, and are prepared to throw themselves into the cut and thrust of community theater. Attracting hordes of society's "passengers" will do us no good at all. Please ensure that anyone you encourage to join is the sort of person who reflects our established values and work ethic.

Who can forget the moment last spring when a colony of semi-rare bats was discovered living in the church hall rafters? Delight soon turned to dismay when we realized their careful eviction would mean the temporary postponement of *An Evening with Gary Lineker* and that sixty-seven-year-old Joyce Walford would have to play the great football hero in his prime. All proceeds from *Jack and the Beanstalk* will go toward replacing parts of the roof that, after all the upheaval, were discovered to be beyond repair. So, please, sell, sell, sell those tickets!

Finally, may I introduce everyone to our new members. In particular Carly and Matthew Dexter, who moved into the largest detached house on Hayward Heights, and the lovely Fran Elroy-Jones, who is the Regional Manager of Sainsbury's. A warm welcome to The Fairway Players!

Celia and Joel Halliday, OBE
The Fairway Players

**Message exchange between Emma Crooks and Celia Halliday on December 3, 2022:**

2:12 p.m. Emma wrote:
LOVE your letter, Celia.

2:18 p.m. Celia wrote:
Thank you, Emma. I do my best for the group. Always have, always will.

2:20 p.m. Emma wrote:
You know there are two more new members? Barry's girlfriend, Myra, and the quiet little man, Dustin.

2:22 p.m. Celia wrote:
Yes, and both are housed on the Grange Estate. Someone who shall remain nameless (despite having two, and a hyphen) did an extended leaflet drop, and they are the result.

2:26 p.m. Emma wrote:
Let's hope they don't cause any trouble that might reflect badly on that person.

2:27 p.m. Celia wrote:
Indeed. We can hope.

---

**Message exchange between Emma Crooks and Sarah-Jane MacDonald on December 3, 2022:**

2:38 p.m. Emma wrote:
Have you seen Celia's email?

2:41 p.m. Sarah-Jane wrote:

Yes, and I'm not rising to it.

2:43 p.m. Emma wrote:

She waits to see what you write, then sends a smug, passive-aggressive reminder to you and everyone else of what you forgot to include.

2:44 p.m. Sarah-Jane wrote:

I didn't forget anything. I've already introduced the new members and mentioned set building at rehearsals. My emails are fully considered and concise.

2:47 p.m. Emma wrote:

Notice how she brings up the postponement whenever she gets the chance?

2:53 p.m. Sarah-Jane wrote:

Yes, and mentions that Joyce had to play Gary Lineker. It speaks only of our ingenuity and resourcefulness, in the face of a dip in the number of active members. I hasten to add that is temporary. If we can mine the Grange Estate and Hayward Heights for newbies, we'll be back to healthy membership levels in no time.

2:54 p.m. Emma wrote:

But what she says about your scenery!

2:59 p.m. Sarah-Jane wrote:

She can say what she likes. I'm proud of the set, and so will everyone else be when the curtain goes up.

---

**Message exchange between Carol Dearing and Sarah-Jane MacDonald on December 3, 2022:**

3:15 p.m. Carol wrote:
Bloody Celia!

3:17 p.m. Sarah-Jane wrote:
Calm down, Mum, ignore her. That's what I do.

---

**Message exchange between Sarah-Jane and Kevin MacDonald on December 3, 2022:**

3:20 p.m. Sarah-Jane wrote:
Bloody Celia! Ever since we introduced committee elections she's been unbearable. She considers herself and Joel, OBE, the spiritual leaders of the group and has never forgiven us for winning the vote. It's democracy, FFS!

3:26 p.m. Kevin wrote:
True, but it was the committee vetoing their choice of spring play that ushered in a new era of mortal offense. Well, we all agreed, farces are old-fashioned. Audiences expect witty, insightful comedy these days, not cheap slapstick.

3:31 p.m. Sarah-Jane wrote:
She hates it that I want every production—even the panto—to be as slick and polished as possible. She and Joel, OBE, deserve an honor for services to jealousy.

3:33 p.m. Kevin wrote:
You're right and, let's face it, only Celia could trash talk a beanstalk.

**Message exchange between Jock Rankin and Joel Halliday, OBE, on December 3, 2022:**

5:38 p.m. Jock wrote:
Beanstalk ok?

5:44 p.m. Joel wrote:
I had no idea that old thing was still around. Thought it was dead and buried.

5:45 p.m. Joel wrote:
Gone for good, I mean.

5:49 p.m. Jock wrote:
They buried it in my lockup! Last to use it were The Minstrel Players for an open-air *Midsummer Night's Dream*. It rained the whole week, and that stalk came back looking like a wet lettuce and smelling of foxes.

5:51 p.m. Joel wrote:
Well, Sarah-Jane is determined to give it a new lease on life.

5:55 p.m. Jock wrote:
Good luck with that.

---

To: Sarah-Jane MacDonald
From: Joyce Walford
Date: December 3, 2022
Subject: That tree

Celia's grumbling behind your back about the size of the beanstalk. She says it should be scrapped. But don't listen to her. If you ask me, it's very impressive and should stay. I remember it from when we did this panto before, years ago. It's a lot more battered and bruised now than it was, but then again, aren't we all? My Nick and Barry will give it a scrub, a coat of paint, and spruce it up for you. Joyce

---

To: Joyce Walford
From: Sarah-Jane MacDonald
Date: December 3, 2022
Subject: Re: That tree

Can they? That would be so helpful. The brighter and newer the beanstalk looks, the better. They're welcome to invoice for paint, brushes, filler—whatever they need. John will reimburse them from group funds.

So the beanstalk has been here before. I remember the group staged *Jack* in the early nineties, but I was a grouchy teenager then and refused to go. Mum has no memory for stage props, and because Helen looked after the albums there are no photos from that time.

That's fine. Actually, it's more than fine. If Celia, or anyone else, should grumble about the beanstalk, we can assure them it's only what the Haywards used in the glory days of The Fairway Players. Thank you, Joyce. Thank you very much. Sarah-Jane MacDonald

---

**Message exchange between Emma Crooks and Sarah-Jane MacDonald on December 4, 2022:**

6:01 p.m. Emma wrote:
I've just arrived for rehearsal and OMG! That beanstalk is AMAZING! Perfect.

6:02 p.m. Sarah-Jane wrote:

Thanks. It needs a bit of TLC, but will be worth it on the night.

---

**Message exchange between Emma Crooks and Celia Halliday on December 4, 2022:**

6:04 p.m. Emma wrote:

OMG! That beanstalk is AWFUL!

6:07 p.m. Celia wrote:

Indeed. But Sarah-Jane insisted. She'll be hoisted on her own petard soon enough, and will only have herself to blame.

---

**Message exchange between Denise Malcolm and Marianne Payne on December 4, 2022:**

7:37 p.m. Denise wrote:

I'm backstage watching the crowd scene. That quiet little man—Dustin. Does he look familiar to you?

7:44 p.m. Marianne wrote:

Never mind him. There's something else familiar around here—that bloody beanstalk!

---

**Message exchange between Celia Halliday and Fran Elroy-Jones on December 4, 2022:**

7:49 p.m. Celia wrote:
I've been watching the opening scenes and you were fabulous, Fran!

7:50 p.m. Fran wrote:
Thank you. I did my best. The beanstalk is quite something.

7:52 p.m. Celia wrote:
Between you and me, the only Fairway Player genuinely impressed by that monstrous old triffid is Woof.

7:52 p.m. Fran wrote:
I saw him scratching around it.

7:53 p.m. Celia wrote:
Fran, do you watch a lot of musical theater?

7:53 p.m. Fran wrote:
Yes, whenever I can—I love it.

7:55 p.m. Celia wrote:
Well, I have two premium tickets to see *The Book of Mormon* in the first week of January. Joel and I can't go now. Are you interested?

7:56 p.m. Fran wrote:
Absolutely! It's one of my favorites—I'd love to see it again. Thank you, Celia. How much do I owe you?

7:59 p.m. Celia wrote:
I don't want any money—only to know the recipients will enjoy the show. It'll be a chance for you and Greg to get to know each other properly.

8:00 p.m. Fran wrote:

You want me to go with your son?

8:01 Celia wrote:

I knew you'd jump at the chance! Tickets will be dispatched in due course.

---

**Message exchange between Dustin Perez and Sarah-Jane MacDonald on December 4, 2022:**

11:22 p.m. Dustin wrote:

I hope you don't mind me texting you so late, Sarah-Jane. May I ask why The Fairway Players had a change of leadership two years ago?

11:22 p.m. Sarah-Jane wrote:

No, you may not.

11:24 p.m. Dustin wrote:

Joyce and Marianne were talking in hushed voices about something "that happened." I just wondered what that was.

11:25 p.m. Sarah-Jane wrote:

The past has no place in the here and now. That's all I'll say on the matter.

11:27 p.m. Dustin wrote:

Oh. In my experience, if the past is buried away, it has a habit of popping up, without warning and when you least expect it.

11:31 p.m. Sarah-Jane wrote:

You're a very competent actor, Dustin, with a natural ability to inhabit a role, however small. I've been a Fairway Player for many years and can spot talent a mile away. Call it stage presence or perhaps a chameleon-like quality, but whatever it is, you have it.

11:33 p.m. Dustin wrote:
Well, thank you, Sarah-Jane. I'm a lifelong practitioner of amateur drama and your approval has made me rather tearful. Thank you.

---

**Message exchange between Sarah-Jane and Kevin MacDonald on December 4, 2022:**

11:40 p.m. Sarah-Jane wrote:
The new chap, Dustin, was asking about "what happened" here. He must've overheard Joyce and Marianne talking about the Haywards. I distracted him with praise for his—genuinely outstanding—acting talent.

11:41 p.m. Kevin wrote:
Good work. We all need to move on. Driving home with Sammy now.

---

**Message exchange between Sarah-Jane MacDonald, Marianne Payne, and Joyce Walford on December 4, 2022:**

11:52 p.m. Sarah-Jane wrote:
Apologies for messaging so late, ladies. Only I understand some cast members have been gossiping about you-know-what. A crime was committed, the wrong person imprisoned, but in the end justice prevailed. As a community, we must move on, and part of that is to let the past slip quietly away. This will be impossible if it keeps being exhumed via whispers and rumor. Believe me, every time something

like that is dug up, it will only look more and more putrid. I therefore politely ask that what happened here in 2018 is not the subject of idle chat in front of new members.

11:52 p.m. Marianne wrote:
We're sorry, SJ. It won't happen again.

11:53 p.m. Joyce wrote:
My poor departed Harry used to say: the past is best buried as deep as you can dig it, and the ground above stamped on.

---

**Message exchange between Fran Elroy-Jones and Karen Payne on December 5, 2022:**

8:19 a.m. Fran wrote:
Karen, I don't wish our working relationship to impact upon the panto, but the shopping cart Simple Simon rides in on—it's one of ours. Did you ask permission to take a cart off-site and, if so, do you have the release form?

8:49 a.m. Karen wrote:
I'm so sorry, Miss Elroy-Jones. It's only an old one that was slung in a corner of the loading bay. It hasn't even been updated with the latest slogan. I thought no one would miss it, and this is basically recycling. Plus, it's free advertising. I can see *The Gazette* review now: "Sainsbury's supports community group"—you can't buy that sort of publicity.

8:50 a.m. Fran wrote:
Well, you really should have asked first. I'll organize the paperwork this morning.

To: Sarah-Jane MacDonald
From: Rev. Joshua Harries
Date: December 5, 2022
Subject: Wall panel

Dear Mrs. MacDonald,

I popped into the church hall this morning to take a sneak peek at the pantomime set and check our wall panel has been properly stored.

Unfortunately, the closer I got to the stage, the more a pungent odor overwhelmed my nostrils . . .

Mrs. MacDonald, there is canine urine on the wall panel and, I suspect, the beanstalk too. There is no pleasanter way to say this.

Please, can I ask that you thoroughly clean and disinfect the panel as a matter of urgency. I must also insist it is untouched for the duration of your rehearsals and performance. The last thing we want is to raise money for the roof, only to have an additional cost of replacing the wall. Yours, Rev. Harries

---

**Message exchange between Sarah-Jane MacDonald and Celia Halliday on December 5, 2022:**

10:06 a.m. Sarah-Jane wrote:
Woof disgraced himself on the beanstalk last night.

10:06 a.m. Celia wrote:
Oh dear.

10:07 a.m. Sarah-Jane wrote:
He's done the same on the wall panel that Father Josh expressly asked us to take care of.

10:08 a.m. Celia wrote:
Well, dealing with problems like that is all part of being in charge.

10:09 a.m. Sarah-Jane wrote:
From now on, Woof is excluded from rehearsals.

10:12 a.m. Celia wrote:
Then Joel and I can't be involved, and I'd say that losing your pantomime dame, key set-builder, and Queen of Cloud Land constitutes a bigger problem than a bit of widdle.

10:15 a.m. Sarah-Jane wrote:
My mum will dog-sit during rehearsals and for play night. Problem solved.

---

**Message exchange between Sarah-Jane MacDonald and Carol Dearing on December 5, 2022:**

10:22 a.m. Sarah-Jane wrote:
Hi, Mum, how are you?

10:23 a.m. Carol wrote:
Why?

10:30 a.m. Sarah-Jane wrote:
There's an issue. Literally, an issue from Woof. He's weed on the church's wall panel and, worst of all, the beanstalk. Luckily the Walford

boys haven't started renovating it yet. I'm mustering all my mettle to clean it off. I've told Celia she can't bring that dog to rehearsals anymore.

10:31 a.m. Carol wrote:
Good job, too. He's nothing but trouble.

10:40 a.m. Sarah-Jane wrote:
Mum, I have a favor to ask.

10:40 a.m. Carol wrote:
No! NO!

10:41 a.m. Sarah-Jane wrote:
Just for a few rehearsals, dress, technical, and play night.

10:42 a.m. Carol wrote:
Absolutely not! He's a monstrous slobbering thing with no brain.

10:44 a.m. Sarah-Jane wrote:
I've said you'll pick him up at six.

---

**Message exchange between Sarah-Jane and Kevin MacDonald on December 5, 2022:**

4:36 p.m. Sarah-Jane wrote:
I've just wiped dog wee off all surfaces below knee-height in the church hall. Celia is savoring the sweet taste of victory, and Mum may never speak to me again.

4:43 p.m. Kevin wrote:
You'll get your reward on play night when the audience gasps, laughs, and cheers. Love you.

4:43 p.m. Sarah-Jane wrote:
Ditto.

---

To: Sarah-Jane MacDonald
From: Marianne Payne
Date: December 6, 2022
Subject: Re: Jack and the Beanstalk

Dear Sarah-Jane, count me, Mick, and Karen in for set building this week. Now, at Sunday's rehearsal you asked if anyone could source bulk orders of sweets to give out at the end of the performance. Well, Mick knows someone who can get his hands on a *lot* of sweets. I know we haven't thrown lollipops into the audience for years—ever since a couple of kiddies lost their eyes—but he can get sweets that are wrapped (so no worries about viruses or germs) and aren't on sticks, for a price that's *very* competitive. Shall I say yes? Marianne, Mick, and Karen xxx

---

To: Marianne Payne
From: Sarah-Jane MacDonald
Date: December 6, 2022
Subject: Re: Jack and the Beanstalk

Excellent news! Ask Mick to order a bag of mixed sweets suitable for a range of ages and tastes. Thank you. I'll source little gift bags and we can hand those out, rather than throw loose sweets—

which only creates a competitive environment where the most aggressive children triumph. Incidentally, no one lost eyes *here*, Marianne; it was a general safety concern among the pantomime community. Please thank Mick and say that I trust him to get the best price possible for the sweets. Sarah-Jane MacDonald

---

To: Sarah-Jane MacDonald
From: Marianne Payne
Date: December 6, 2022
Subject: Re: Jack and the Beanstalk

You know Mick—he'll get the best price! I'd just like to mention that Karen was a little bit disappointed in her nonspeaking role. She'd never mention it to you herself, but as her mum, I will. She loves panto and that's why she asked her boss Fran to come and audition. She also acquired an old shopping cart for Harley to use as Simple Simon, so it seems a bit of a shame that Fran ended up with the lead role, while Karen is merely a Common Villager. This is so that you know Karen is happy to take on a bigger part, if anything should become available. I notice the well-to-do couple haven't been back, and yet their characters actually have names. Love, Marianne xxx

---

To: Carly & Matthew Dexter
From: Sarah-Jane MacDonald
Date: December 6, 2022
Subject: The Fairway Players

Dear Carly and Matthew,
It was an absolute pleasure to meet you both at the auditions two weeks ago. I can't tell you how delighted I am to welcome you to

The Fairway Players. We are a well-established, friendly group committed to delivering quality entertainment to the local community. Do you know your beautiful new house is actually built on the site of Hayward Heights, a house that used to belong to our founding members, Martin and Helen Hayward? It must be fate that you should decide to join the group as soon as you arrive!

However, since you came to the audition and introduced yourselves, we haven't seen you again. In your absence, you have been cast in our pantomime as Buxom Betty (Carly) and Mr. Ugly the Village Idiot (Matthew). Apologies for the names; this panto was written in the 1970s and we are retaining the authenticity of the script. Please be assured both are the most prestigious of the smaller roles. It would be lovely if you could let me know you're still interested, and start coming to rehearsals, so you learn your part and our ladies can measure you for costumes.

We hold set building afternoons every Sunday and, if you have any questions, please do not hesitate to contact me. Sarah-Jane MacDonald

---

To: Sarah-Jane MacDonald
From: Myra Briggs
Date: December 8, 2022
Subject: Panto

hi am I in the panto havent heard and barry dont know coz he forgot his email pword the plonker love im really im bit scared but dont know if I got a part or not im a teaching assistant at lockwood primary myra

---

To: Myra Briggs
From: Sarah-Jane MacDonald
Date: December 8, 2022
Subject: Re: Panto

You're a Common Villager.
Sarah-Jane MacDonald

---

**Message exchange between Emma Crooks and Sarah-Jane MacDonald on December 8, 2022:**

7:04 a.m. Emma wrote:
I offered to give leaflets to my yoga class at the Grange Community Hub, but Celia said we aren't targeting "those people." Is that true?

7:21 a.m. Sarah-Jane wrote:
As elected chair of the group, I'm happy to take anyone's ticket money for the good cause of the church hall roof.

---

**Message exchange between Emma Crooks and Celia Halliday on December 8, 2022:**

7:25 a.m. Emma wrote:
I asked her and she said yes.

7:31 a.m. Celia wrote:
I see. Well, the food bank is open from eight until two. Perhaps give away some leaflets there? It would be lovely to reach all the local children.

---

**Message exchange between Dustin Perez and Fran Elroy-Jones on December 8, 2022:**

10:32 p.m. Dustin wrote:
From one newbie to another: congratulations on getting the part of "princess."

10:32 p.m. Fran wrote:
Thanks, you too. What part do you play?

10:34 p.m. Dustin wrote:
I'm one of the Giant's Fairies. How did you come to join?

10:40 p.m. Fran wrote:
In her appraisal Karen mentioned this is her hobby, and then a leaflet came through the door. I'm new at work and I've just moved here, so want to meet people. Totally didn't think I'd be cast in a leading role. I'm quite nervous. You?

10:41 p.m. Dustin wrote:
Same. New to the area and want to meet people.

10:41 p.m. Fran wrote:
They seem a friendly, harmonious group.

10:42 p.m. Dustin wrote:
Yes, they certainly seem to be.

**Charlotte**
Mr. Tanner strikes again. No idea what he's getting at.

**Femi**
I have a page of notes.

**Charlotte**
Really? Shit.

**Femi**
There's been a shift in the politics of the group. Sarah-Jane and Kevin are now the power couple.

**Charlotte**
At the top of the beanstalk.

**Femi**
But unlike the Haywards, they don't have the absolute power of this being *their* group. They have to retain their popularity with the rank and file, or be voted out.

**Charlotte**
Uneasy lies the head that wears the crown.

**Femi**
Celia and Joel.

**Charlotte**

As friends of the Haywards, their social standing was assured. Now they have to find new ways to stay on top. It's brought out a ruthlessly competitive streak in Celia. I don't recall her being quite like this when we examined the Lockwood case before.

**Femi**

She's waiting for SJ to fall from grace. Complains about the beanstalk. Doesn't want the pantomime to benefit from Fran's musical connections.

**Charlotte**

It's as if she's torn between her need to appear loyal to The Fairway Players—mindful of future committee elections—and actively orchestrate problems for Sarah-Jane and Kevin.

**Femi**

She undermines SJ whenever she can do it subtly. Her campaign is one of quiet sabotage.

**Charlotte**

There's at least one game-player in the mix. Emma is determined to be in favor with whoever rules the roost. She's SJ's confidante, but behind her back is sycophantic to Celia. If the power couple changes, she'll still be "in."

**Femi**

The group is a young democracy. In any situation of change, the old guard can be reluctant to move on. Is Sarah-Jane right: that past events shouldn't be mentioned?

**Charlotte**

I don't know, but that brings us to the new members.

**Femi**

Two new estates: a private one and public housing. More houses mean an expanding community.

**Charlotte**

Greater demographic diversity, a disruption of the status quo and a dilution of power—for some.

**Femi**

Who may see it as a threat. Celia isn't interested in recruiting new members from the housing estate, while seeming desperate to recruit the residents of Hayward Heights.

**Charlotte**

And for all her faults, Sarah-Jane seems happy to build their membership from both, and to grow the drama group in ways they couldn't, with the established community.

**Femi**
But what's the mystery, and why has Mr. Tanner involved us again?

To: Sarah-Jane MacDonald
From: Victoria Mayhew
Date: December 9, 2022
Subject: Jack and the Beanstalk

Dear Sarah-Jane,

My eight-year-old attends Lockwood Prep and today brought home a leaflet for *Jack and the Beanstalk*. Before we decide, as a family, to attend this event, can I ask:

1.  Is the group committed to recycling, with the aim of net-zero emissions?
2.  Is the environment gender-neutral?
3.  Is there a trigger-warning for language, characters, or ideology?
4.  Is the group aware of recent data protection laws, given that your personal email address appears on this leaflet?
5.  Is the group committed to sustainable banking?
6.  Are food products in the room allergen-free?
7.  Are edibles wrapped and guaranteed free from bacteria and viruses?
8.  What time does the show start?

I look forward to hearing from you at your earliest convenience.

Victoria Mayhew
She/her

To: Victoria Mayhew
From: Sarah-Jane MacDonald
Date: December 9, 2022
Subject: Re: Jack and the Beanstalk

Dear Victoria,

I am happy to supply answers as follows:

1. We are reusing a forty-year-old beanstalk.
2. Pantomime is the original gender-fluid theater.
3. It was written in the 1970s.
4. My email address is the contact point for anything related to The Fairway Players.
5. Our treasurer is a retired accountant.
6. No. If you're allergic to cakes and fruit chews, bring your EpiPen.
7. Yes. Children will take home a goodie bag of wrapped sweets.
8. 6 p.m.

If you have any further questions, please do not hesitate to ask.

Sarah-Jane MacDonald
She/her

---

**Message from Jade's phone to Sarah-Jane MacDonald on December 9, 2022:**

3:03 p.m. Jade's phone wrote:
Aaaliyah picked up a flyer for jack and the beanstalk outside the food bank. I run a new childcare group on the public housing estate. The kids would love to come is it free?

**Message posted to The Fairway Players' Committee's WhatsApp group on December 9, 2022:**

**Sarah-Jane**

Can whoever is handing out leaflets to families exiting the food bank please desist. It gives the impression the tickets are free. Of course I'd love everyone to see the show, regardless of income, but this panto is to raise money for the church roof and we must prioritize paying customers. STRICTLY NO FREEBIES. NO EXCEPTIONS.

---

**Message exchange between Sarah-Jane MacDonald and Jade's phone on December 9, 2022:**

3:26 p.m. Sarah-Jane wrote:
Ok, just this once. I hope Aaliyah enjoys the show.

3:33 p.m. Jade's phone wrote:
Yes! We're both dancing around the room, so happy. Thanks, Sarah, we really appreciate this. Oh, and it's Aaaliyah with three a's. They stand for: awesome, amazing, and August.

3:35 p.m. Sarah-Jane wrote:
Aaaliyah it is . . . I assume August is the month she was born?

3:41 p.m. Jade's phone wrote:
It's the month HE was born.

3:43 p.m. Sarah-Jane wrote:
Text me when you arrive, I'll let you and Aaaliyah in.

**Message exchange between Sarah-Jane MacDonald and Branded Solutions [Orders] Ltd. on December 9, 2022:**

3:50 p.m. Sarah-Jane wrote:
I placed an order on December 6 for twenty-five girls' Christmas gift bags and twenty-five boys' Christmas gift bags. Please can I change it to fifty gender-neutral Christmas gift bags? It's occurred to me we should move with the times.

3:52 p.m. Branded Solutions [Orders] Ltd. wrote:
No problem. I'll change that for you. They'll arrive next week.

---

To: Sarah-Jane MacDonald
From: Kevin MacDonald
Date: December 9, 2022
Subject: Draft program

Finalizing the program now. A few questions: Have the Dexters accepted their roles? We haven't seen them since the audition. Are we changing the name of Callous Hands? It refers to the then–prime minister James Callaghan and his high tax rates, but no one under sixty will get the joke, and anyone over sixty won't remember. Also, does saying the Giant is just a voice give away the fact that we never see him? Likewise, revealing in the program that Mick is both the Bean Dealer and the King of Cloud Land is a bit of a spoiler for that final twist, no? Thoughts?

---

**Message exchange between Sarah-Jane and Kevin MacDonald on December 9, 2022:**

4:11 p.m. Sarah-Jane wrote:
Names etc. can stay the same. It's what appeared in the original West End production in 1978. Authenticity. Integrity of the text, and all that.

4:12 p.m. Kevin wrote:
It's a pantomime. It has zero integrity.

4:15 p.m. Sarah-Jane wrote:
The Hallidays changed all the F-words in *Glengarry Glen Ross* to "fiddle." We're not the Hallidays.

4:15 p.m. Kevin wrote:
And the Dexters?

4:16 p.m. Sarah-Jane wrote:
Yes, they're on board. I'm sure. Just print the sheet.

4:17 p.m. Kevin wrote:
Good. Good to know you're as speechless with thanks, as ever.

4:20 p.m. Sarah-Jane wrote:
Thank you, Keith, for your hard work on this production.

4:22 p.m. Kevin wrote:
We've been married for eighteen years. For fiddle's sake—it's Kevin!

4:23 p.m. Sarah-Jane wrote:
Sorry, autocorrect.

---

To: The Fairway Players' mailing list
From: Sarah-Jane MacDonald
Date: December 11, 2022
Subject: Set building and rehearsal

Dear all,

Thank you to everyone who turned up at the church hall today for set building and a late-afternoon rehearsal. We don't have long now before curtain-up and I'm delighted to say some cast members are forging ahead and learning their words. A particular mention must go to Emma, Harley, and Fran, who are all off book and already developing their characters.

Every day is a school day and I learned something interesting this week. Our spectacular beanstalk has trod these very boards before. In the early nineties the group's founders selected it for one of The Fairway Players' first pantomimes. While I firmly believe the past should not dictate the present, sometimes it can peek around the door and give you a thumbs-up on your decision. This is one of those moments.

I hope those of you who remember the beanstalk do so with fondness in your hearts and that its presence here now ignites your passion for this production, which I intend to be the best pantomime the group has ever staged.

Our next evening rehearsal will be Wednesday.

Sarah-Jane MacDonald
Director of *Jack and the Beanstalk* and cochair of The Fairway Players

To: The Fairway Players' mailing list
From: Celia Halliday
Date: December 11, 2022
Subject: Hello, old friend!

Dear all,

Well, those of us who are long-standing members of the group will have said a cautious "hello" to an old friend yesterday. The over-large beanstalk that now dominates our stage, and all who tread upon it, has in fact appeared here once before.

It was the early 1990s and the Haywards staged the most bril-liant production of *Jack* I've ever seen. A production that simply could never be bettered. However, I remember a consensus at the time being that the beanstalk was a terrible folly we didn't need, and would have spoiled the production, were it not for the quality of the performances and the live music, played by a professional band.

And that was when this ancient relic was fairly new. Heaven only knows where it's been since we waved a relieved farewell to it thirty years ago! We can but hope our wonderful performances will sim-ilarly distract from the fact it now smells like a pensioner's carpet.

Celia Halliday
The Fairway Players

---

To: The Fairway Players' mailing list
From: Sarah-Jane MacDonald
Date: December 11, 2022
Subject: Re: Set building and rehearsal

In my last email I forgot to mention that Joyce has volunteered her sons, Nick and Barry, to revamp the beanstalk with a deep clean, filler, paint, varnish, and general TLC. I have been assured they will be working their magic over the next couple of days. That beanstalk will be a stunning centerpiece for a stunning production we can all be proud of.

Sarah-Jane MacDonald
Director of *Jack and the Beanstalk* and cochair of The Fairway Players

---

**Message exchange between Carol Dearing and Sarah-Jane MacDonald on December 12, 2022:**

11:11 p.m. Carol wrote:
I'm fuming and I'm not the only one. How dare she imply your production won't be as good as the last time—thirty-one years ago!! That woman really puts the BS in Jack and the BS.

11:15 p.m. Sarah-Jane wrote:
Calm down, Mum. Everyone will love the BS once it's cleaned up. All it needs is some cosmetic attention, no more.

---

To: Sarah-Jane MacDonald
From: Denise Malcolm
Date: December 12, 2022
Subject: The beanstalk

Dear Sarah-Jane, Celia is quite right—that beanstalk *has* appeared on this stage before. Martin directed and Helen was Jack—this same big thing towered over us all. Martin said "never again" a few times! You do know it's made of asbestos, don't you? Denise

---

**Message exchange between Sarah-Jane and Kevin MacDonald on December 12, 2022:**

8:18 a.m. Sarah-Jane wrote:

I know you're driving, but I've just had a worrying email from Denise. The beanstalk might be made from asbestos.

8:29 a.m. Kevin wrote:

Shit! Yes, in car. On voice. Asbestos ok, so long as we don't break it up and release dust. Nick filled in any splits the day we installed it. It's safe. Don't panic. All good.

8:31 a.m. Sarah-Jane wrote:

I know the facts, but people are paranoid. We won't get another beanstalk as impressive as this at such short notice. No one must know it contains asbestos. Will brief Denise. DON'T TELL ANYONE.

---

To: Denise Malcolm
From: Sarah-Jane MacDonald
Date: December 12, 2022
Subject: All fine!

Dear Denise,

Yes, the beanstalk is already familiar to some of our longer-standing members. How wonderful that it's been here before, and now a new generation of players can enjoy acting alongside it. The circle of life is right here on our stage.

Denise, a polite request. The rumors of asbestos are really not helpful to the harmonious progression of rehearsals—not to mention ticket sales, on which the production and its very worthy charity (the church hall roof) rely.

Even *if* it contains *some* asbestos, and it's by no means certain, there really is no danger at all to The Fairway Players or our audience. That noxious substance is only deadly when its dust is released and inhaled.

If you're happy to keep all mention of the A-word to yourself, I'm more than prepared to consider you for the much higher-profile nonspeaking role of Buxom Betty—if Carly Dexter decides she doesn't want to be involved after all. Yours hopefully, Sarah-Jane MacDonald

---

To: Carly & Matthew Dexter
From: Sarah-Jane MacDonald
Date: December 12, 2022
Subject: The Fairway Players

Dear Carly and Matthew,
I've just swung past your beautiful house to see if you were in. Yes, that was me looking through the mail slot, then the porch window, then the lounge window, and then sourcing an old crate from the yard next door and standing on it, to see over the back gate. At that point I noticed you have video cameras trained all over the front of the house. Please be assured I wasn't snooping, merely concerned that your bell wasn't working.

I noticed your mail piled up on the mat, and that might explain why I haven't received a reply from you regarding your roles in The Fairway Players' panto, *Jack and the Beanstalk*. Perhaps you've been called away urgently and haven't been able to respond?

Rehearsals are well under way and I very much look forward to welcoming you at one of them soon. Very best wishes, Sarah-Jane MacDonald

**Message exchange between Sarah-Jane MacDonald and Carol Dearing on December 12, 2022:**

11:34 p.m. Sarah-Jane wrote:
Mum, can you pop around and see if the Dexters are in now? It could be they keep late hours and I'm just going around at the wrong times. They live on Hayward Heights in the big, double-fronted, two-story, mock-Georgian country house with a CCTV camera, a Tesla charging point, and two Doric columns holding up a pediment.

11:38 p.m. Carol wrote:
Why can't you go?

11:44 p.m. Sarah-Jane wrote:
I'm exhausted after sorting out the Christmas food list and dragging decorations down from the loft. Kevin's been looking after Sammy all day and they're both fast asleep. Harley is in his room. I don't want to disturb them all by going out. And you live so much nearer than I do.

11:46 p.m. Carol wrote:
I'm in my nightie. And what am I supposed to say when I get there? "Merry Christmas"?

11:47 p.m. Sarah-Jane wrote:
You could ask why they auditioned for the panto—competently enough to secure key nonspeaking roles—but haven't come to rehearsals, or contacted us, ever since.

11:49 p.m. Carol wrote:
No! Go to sleep.

To: Sarah-Jane MacDonald
From: Dustin Perez
Date: December 13, 2022
Subject: A delicate matter

Dear Sarah-Jane,

I want to speak to you on a delicate matter. This is my first time with The Fairway Players—though I've acted with drama groups of all persuasions around the UK—so I hope I'm not speaking out of turn. Only, I overheard some conversations during the tea break yesterday and the subject matter was very worrying indeed. I'm in two minds whether to tell you or not. I don't want to fan the flames of gossip. But then again, perhaps you *ought* to know. It affects the group, and the production, after all. Do you *want* to know? Dustin

---

To: Dustin Perez
From: Sarah-Jane MacDonald
Date: December 13, 2022
Subject: Re: A delicate matter

Dear Dustin,

I know very well what the rumors are, and I'm happy to quash them.

The truth is our beanstalk *may* contain something nasty. It was constructed in the early eighties and was designed to be fire-retardant—as everything used in stage scenery must be. Asbestos is a mineral fiber mixed with other composites to form a strong material that's resistant to heat and corrosion. I can send the Wikipedia links to anyone in doubt.

Any asbestos that *may* be in the beanstalk is firmly sealed away and, thanks to the Walford boys, will be freshly painted into place. It is perfectly safe to be around—so long as no one breaks open the trunk and ingests any microfibers that are released as a result. There is absolutely no danger to our cast, crew, or audience. No pesky pathogens will escape on my watch!

However, I very much appreciate your email, Dustin. It is useful to know that rumors have been going around, despite my attempts to keep them in check. I'll address anyone else's concerns as and when they arise. Sarah-Jane MacDonald

---

To: Sarah-Jane MacDonald
From: Dustin Perez
Date: December 13, 2022
Subject: Re: A delicate matter

The beanstalk is made of asbestos? Oh my goodness, that's shocking news! I had an uncle die of mesothelioma. If you don't mind, Sarah-Jane, I won't go anywhere near it onstage. My character will have to sing and dance downstage left. I'd never withdraw from a production this late, but if I'd known there were toxic props in this panto, I'd have done *Oh! What a Lovely War* with the Mendham Players.

---

To: Dustin Perez
From: Sarah-Jane MacDonald
Date: December 13, 2022
Subject: Re: A delicate matter

Well, what was the "delicate matter" you overheard, if not that?

---

To: Sarah-Jane MacDonald
From: Dustin Perez
Date: December 13, 2022
Subject: Re: A delicate matter

It was just that, according to a couple of people, there's a convicted murderer in Lockwood. They're out of prison and have been spotted in town.

---

To: Dustin Perez
From: Sarah-Jane MacDonald
Date: December 13, 2022
Subject: Re: A delicate matter

Is that all? Phew! Let me assure you, Dustin, that is light relief compared to everything else that's going on at the moment. Please, please, please do not mention the little "asbestos" problem. I promise you can stay away from the beanstalk if you wish. And perhaps you'd like to be Mr. Ugly the Village Idiot instead of your lesser, nonspeaking role? You'd be absolutely perfect. This is, if the Dexters don't come back. It would be good to have an ugly idiot on standby. Sarah-Jane MacDonald

---

**Handwritten note delivered to Mr. & Mrs. Dexter, 14 Hayward Heights, on December 14, 2022:**

Dear Carly and Matthew, I'm afraid that if I don't hear from you by 7 p.m. on Friday December 16 I will be obliged to give your roles to other actors. It would be such a shame, as we are desperate for good, solid members like yourselves, but I have to think of the production and allow your understudies to rehearse their parts.

Please contact me at your earliest convenience.
Sarah-Jane MacDonald

---

To: Joyce Walford
From: Sarah-Jane MacDonald
Date: December 14, 2022
Subject: Thank you

Joyce, I take back everything I've ever said about your boys. The beanstalk looks *fabulous*. They've cleaned it up, scaled the chipped sections with filler, painted, and varnished the whole thing. It looks as good as new. I'm stunned. I wasn't expecting a job as good as that. Sarah Jane MacDonald

---

To: Sarah-Jane MacDonald
From: Joyce Walford
Date: December 14, 2022
Subject: Re: Thank you

Course they did a good job. It's in the blood. Their dad was a painter and decorator. Lucky for everyone that's all they take after him for.

Sarah-Jane, something you should know: I've sold a ticket. My library friend, Elsie. She's never seen an amateur play before. She usually goes to the Royal Festival Hall for classical concerts and is the nervous sort. I said you'd meet her at the door, give her a history of theater, then show her to her seat and have a chat, so she's not on her own. You can collect a cup of tea for her on the way—I can't leave the kitchen counter, I'll be too busy.

Anyway, what is it you've said about Nick and Barry that you want to take back? Everyone has a downer on them, but my boys are the lights of my life. Joyce

---

To: Joyce Walford
From: Sarah-Jane MacDonald
Date: December 14, 2022
Subject: Re: Thank you

I'll be far too busy to show anyone to their seat, Joyce, let alone give them a history of theater. We have a front-of-house team for that. Or we should have. In fact, would Elsie like to join the front-of-house team? Sarah-Jane MacDonald

---

To: Carol Dearing
From: Sarah-Jane MacDonald
Date: December 16, 2022
Subject: Play week

I'm compiling a system of spreadsheets to organize play week. If ever there were starker evidence our membership is declining, it is this. We have even fewer members to help out with little jobs. Everyone has so many chores at this time of year. The Dexters haven't responded, so I'm moving other actors into their roles, which leaves two nonspeaking parts to fill and I'll probably have to draft Kevin and myself into those. We need a front-of-house team and there aren't any people to spare.

Mum, do you know *anyone* who could dress up as Father Christmas? Santa comes out from backstage at the end of the panto every year, without fail. Joyce's Harry did it for as long as I can remember. I'd completely forgotten he died back in January. I'd ask Joel, but then Celia would know I've neglected a key Fairway tradition. John could do it, but he's Callous Hands the Wage Snatcher, and the children will assume it's the baddie in disguise. Kevin would step up, I know, but I'd rather he go straight home after curtain call to extract Sammy from the babysitter before her fee doubles. I could ask Mick Payne, but this year our audience will include children from Hayward Heights. Most go to the Montessori or the prep and their parents would appreciate a more articulate, educated Santa. Any ideas? Sarah-Jane MacDonald

---

To: Sarah-Jane MacDonald
From: Carol Dearing
Date: December 16, 2022
Subject: Re: Play week

Yes. I'll be Santa. Problem solved. Now, have you done your Christmas round-robin yet? It's been two weeks since Celia sent hers. Mum x

---

To: Sarah-Jane MacDonald
From: Marianne Payne
Date: December 16, 2022
Subject: Sweets

Dear Sarah-Jane, Good news! Mick's friend has got the sweets. He'll drop them at your house about 5 p.m. on play night. I said that's fine. Trouble is, John won't pay him until after Christmas, so I said you'd pay when he drops them off. Cash. I've given him your number. Lots of love, Marianne, Mick, and Karen xxxx

---

To: Marianne Payne
From: Sarah-Jane MacDonald
Date: December 16, 2022
Subject: Re: Sweets

I'll need the sweets long before 5 p.m. on play night. We've got to divide them up and sort them into gender-neutral gift bags. I'll have a hundred other things to do that night, and so will Kevin. As director and producer, we shouldn't really be onstage ourselves, but we'll have to fill in as fairy villagers, else Cloud Land will look like a ghost town. I suppose Harley can sort them in the greenroom in between cueing the music and nipping onstage as Simple Simon. We'll work something out. Thanks, Marianne. Sarah-Jane MacDonald

---

**Message exchange between Sarah-Jane MacDonald and Karen Payne on December 16, 2022:**

7:01 p.m. Sarah-Jane wrote:
Karen, there's a problem with Carly Dexter being Buxom Betty. Will you do it? The character has a "raucous laugh" and a "cheeky titter" to deliver front of stage, so it shouldn't be too taxing for you to learn. Sorry about the name. The script was written in the seventies.

7:02 p.m. Karen wrote:
That's a great big YES!! I'd love to, Sarah-Jane. I'll start learning it now.

---

**Message exchange between Sarah-Jane MacDonald and Dustin Perez on December 16, 2022:**

7:03 p.m. Sarah-Jane wrote:
May I consider you the ugly idiot?

7:03 p.m. Dustin wrote:
You may.

---

**Message exchange between Sarah-Jane and Harley MacDonald on December 17, 2022:**

1:57 p.m. Sarah-Jane wrote:
Darling, sorry to message while you're out with your friends, but have you got the Spotify playlist ready?

1:58 p.m. Harley wrote:
YES

1:58 p.m. Sarah-Jane wrote:
Could a buffering glitch create dead air onstage? Can't help wondering if CDs might be more reliable.

1:59 p.m. Harley wrote:
shut up

---

**Message exchange between Sarah-Jane and Kevin MacDonald on December 17, 2022:**

1:59 p.m. Sarah-Jane wrote:
Harley just told me to shut up.

1:59 p.m. Kevin wrote:
Let me handle it.

---

**Message exchange between Kevin and Harley MacDonald on December 17, 2022:**

2:03 p.m. Kevin wrote:
Don't be rude to your mum. Comprendo, compadre, but she's got a lot on her plate, she works hard and, let's face it, she's the only mum you've got.

2:04 p.m. Harley wrote:
fuck off dad

---

**Message exchange between Kevin and Sarah-Jane MacDonald on December 17, 2022:**

2:05 p.m. Kevin wrote:
All fine. He's sorry. Just worried about school tests and a bit snappy.

2:05 p.m. Sarah-Jane wrote:
Appreciated.

---

To: The Fairway Players' mailing list
From: Sarah-Jane MacDonald
Date: December 18, 2022
Subject: Big Sunday

Dear all,

Play week dawns, and rehearsals for *Jack and the Beanstalk* are in full swing. May I remind you that today is what The Fairway

Players affectionately call Big Sunday. We arrive at the church hall for midday, spend all afternoon finishing the set, then rehearse until the play is good enough to put before a paying audience—however late that may be. It's tiring, but nonetheless essential if the production is to be a success.

Unfortunately, the lovely Dexter couple can no longer take up their roles, so Karen and Dustin have valiantly agreed to step up. That leaves a few gaps in the ensemble, which Kevin and I will fill on the night.

While cast and crew are busy learning lines and cues onstage, our publicity team has been reaching out to the local community. They've approached children and parents at Lockwood Primary and Lockwood Prep to hand out leaflets and sell tickets. As a result—cue drumroll, please—the production is SOLD OUT! Huge thanks to Denise, Marianne, Celia, and Beth for all their hard work.

Finally, a reminder of the good cause that will benefit from this fundraising production. The church hall in Lockwood is where The Fairway Players have staged their plays for nearly forty years. It is our home. This spring it was discovered that a family of bats had inadvertently wreaked havoc when their urine and feces built up in a roof cavity, which was damp from a water leak the previous spring. This perfect storm nurtured a destructive fungus that ate the wooden beams. The hall had to be closed for two weeks while the bats were humanely evicted, a giant patty of petrified dung was cut out, and the damage patched up. Hopefully, any money we raise this week will ensure that whole section of roof can be replaced.

I've seen how hard everyone has worked and I know *Jack and the Beanstalk* will be our best, most successful pantomime yet—all that remains for me to say now is: break a leg for play week!

Sarah-Jane MacDonald
Director of *Jack and the Beanstalk* and cochair of The Fairway Players

---

**Message exchange between Kevin and Sarah-Jane MacDonald on December 18, 2022:**

10:09 a.m. Kevin wrote:
Way, way too much info.

10:11 a.m. Sarah-Jane wrote:
Check today's spreadsheet: remotivate group re church hall roof. I'm reminding everyone what we're working toward. Sometimes you have to be blunt to engage brains.

10:12 a.m. Kevin wrote:
A "patty" of dung. Is that the word?

10:14 a.m. Sarah-Jane wrote:
The bat-conservation people said "a petrified patty of feces." I suppose it's like a cow "pat."

10:14 a.m. Kevin wrote:
Is it feces or faeces?

10:17 a.m. Sarah-Jane wrote:
It's SHIT, Kevin. But if I put that in my rallying email, Celia would complain to the committee. She'll send her own counter-email any second now, you'll see.

To: The Fairway Players' mailing list
From: Celia Halliday
Date: December 18, 2022
Subject: Big Sunday

Dear Fairway Players,

Well, it's here! Play week has arrived and it's time for our hard work, late nights, and furious line-learning to blossom into a fully formed production. This is the moment everything we've been working toward comes together for the all-too-brief seconds we're onstage with the audience's rapt attention in our grasp. When the energy, joy, and passion in the room reaches its beautiful, yet fleeting crescendo.

I won't bore you with tedious detail like minor cast changes. Nor will I spoil your dinner with talk of unmentionable things, and money. This week is all about the magic of Christmas, the history we forge with every play we produce, the love we have for drama . . . it's about the alchemy of the stage.

Fairway Players, this week is about you, the audience, and the great theatrical tradition of pantomime. Enjoy!

Celia Halliday
The Fairway Players

---

**Message exchange between Carol Dearing and Sarah-Jane MacDonald on December 18, 2022:**

10:40 a.m. Carol wrote:
Bloody Celia! I MUCH preferred your email.

10:44 a.m. Sarah-Jane wrote:

Thanks. Can I bring Sammy around to yours this afternoon? I was going to take her to Big Sunday, but I know what she's like. She'll be on the go all day.

10:50 a.m. Carol wrote:

Of course! She's just like you were. Bring her as soon as you like. We'll walk Woof around the park while you're rehearsing.

---

**Message exchange between Denise Malcolm and Sarah-Jane MacDonald on December 18, 2022:**

11:50 a.m. Denise wrote:

You said if I kept quiet about the asbestos I could be Buxom Betty. I've just heard you've given the part to Karen.

11:54 a.m. Sarah-Jane wrote:

Sorry, Denise, but it's not as if I promised. The Paynes have been so helpful for this production. Marianne has sold more tickets than anyone, Karen brought a shopping cart from work, and Mick sourced cheap sweets for the goodie bags.

11:59 a.m. Sarah-Jane wrote:

Look, if anything else comes up, you'll be the first person I think of.

---

To: Sarah-Jane MacDonald
From: Joyce Walford
Date: December 18, 2022
Subject: Re: Big Sunday

I've bought the ingredients for my Christmas cupcakes and festive fruit slices. Last year you and Kevin got the tinsel and streamers for the cake stall, will you do that this year, too? Also, can you bring a sign that says cakes are a dollar each, or two and a half dollars for three; slices are eighty-five cents each, but three dollars for three. I know that makes it more expensive to buy three, but I won't be making as many slices as usual because I lost a baking tin back in June, so I want to stop people buying too many at once. Make the sign nice and big, so everyone can see it. Joyce

---

To: Joyce Walford
From: Sarah-Jane MacDonald
Date: December 18, 2022
Subject: Re: Big Sunday

Thanks, Joyce, but that will look like we made a mistake on our sign. It's unprofessional. I'm unlocking the hall for Big Sunday, so we'll chat later. Sarah-Jane MacDonald

---

**Message exchange between Kevin and Sarah-Jane MacDonald on December 18, 2022:**

2:13 p.m. Kevin wrote:

Don't want to say anything in case you don't agree—united before the troops, and all that—but I've got a great view up here in the lighting box. Should Myra be further forward in this scene, and the new little chap further back?

2:27 p.m. Sarah-Jane wrote:

Dustin won't go near the killer beanstalk, so his movements are confined to downstage left. This is Myra's first-ever stage role. She's terrified and won't venture beyond an arm's length of the wings. The others have dotted themselves about to create the appearance of a bustling crowd.

2:30 p.m. Kevin wrote:

Bustling? They look like Stonehenge.

---

**Message exchange between Celia and Joel Halliday on December 18:**

3:07 p.m. Celia wrote:

This monolithic beanstalk has to be in every scene—including BEFORE the magic beans have even been sown. At the end, Jack pretends to cut a branch off, when the script clearly says he chops the whole thing down. It completely ruins the story. Authenticity, my foot!

3:11 p.m. Joel wrote:

And it's been painted so many times the trapdoor is completely sealed up.

3:15 p.m. Celia wrote:
The beanstalk has a trapdoor?

3:28 p.m. Joel wrote:
Remember, that's why Martin rented it all those years ago. He'd seen it in the West End and wanted our Fairy Godmother to look out from inside the beanstalk. An alternative to hoisting her on a wire—or having her zoom in on an electric scooter, as Beth does now.

3:29 p.m. Celia wrote:
Yes. That rings a bell. Interesting.

---

**Message exchange between Kevin and Sarah-Jane MacDonald on December 18, 2022:**

5:28 p.m. Kevin wrote:
Is Daisy the Cow ok? She appears to be doing the Macarena on the lower slopes of the beanstalk.

5:29 p.m. Sarah-Jane wrote:
That's Nick and Barry Walford in a cow costume.

5:29 p.m. Kevin wrote:
Have they been drinking?

5:30 p.m. Sarah-Jane wrote:
I've just checked and yes, they have. But at least they're not fighting.

---

**Message exchange between Denise Malcolm and Celia Halliday on December 18, 2022:**

6:18 p.m. Denise wrote:

I've heard something Sarah-Jane doesn't want anyone else to know. Something so explosive it could kill this production stone-dead.

6:29 p.m. Celia wrote:

"Evil happens when good people do nothing." You have a whistle, Denise, and a duty to blow it.

6:33 p.m. Denise wrote:

I've had bit-parts and backstage roles for thirty-five years. I want to act. Finally show what I can do. You and Joel are directing the spring play. Can you promise me the female lead? PROMISE, mind.

6:34 p.m. Celia wrote:
I promise.

6:34 p.m. Denise wrote:
The beanstalk is made of asbestos.

6:41 p.m. Celia wrote:

You did the right thing. But don't say anything for the moment, especially as Big Sunday is almost over. We don't want panic in the ranks—yet.

---

To: John O'Dea
From: Celia Halliday
Date: December 19, 2022
Subject: Insurance

Dear John,

A quick word in the strictest confidence. As treasurer of The Fairway Players, you purchase insurance against the group having to cancel a play. Now, back when I was assistant secretary, I remember we opted for a cheaper policy that meant the production was insured up to play night, but if it was called off on the day itself, or if the audience ask for their money back *after* the show, we weren't insured. Can you let me know if that's still the case? Celia

---

To: Celia Halliday
From: John O'Dea
Date: December 19, 2022
Subject: Re: Insurance

It is.
John

---

**Message exchange between Celia Halliday and Denise Malcolm on December 19, 2022:**

12:41 p.m. Celia wrote:
That little matter we spoke about yesterday. Please keep it to yourself for a while longer.

1:15 p.m. Denise wrote:
Ok. What play will I be lead in?

1:27 p.m. Celia wrote:

It should have been *When Did You Last See Your Trousers?* by Ray Galton and John Antrobus. Only someone who shall remain nameless (despite writing it in full at the end of every email) vetoed our plans because, apparently, farce is out of fashion. Instead we've chosen a new version of *The Hound of the Baskervilles.* It was a smash hit in the West End earlier this year.

1:33 p.m. Denise wrote:

Thanks, Celia. My lips are sealed.

---

To: Sarah-Jane MacDonald
From: Carol Dearing
Date: December 21, 2022
Subject: Have you got a beard?

I wrestled this Santa suit from the wardrobe. It is *sans* beard. Any ideas where last year's beard might be? The tunic is far too big. It looks like a summer dress with a loose belt. I might ask Denise to take it in, if she's got time. I'm not wearing these huge shoes with the silver paper buckles. I've got a pair of pixie boots from Next—they'll do. You'll see my ensemble at dress rehearsal tomorrow. Mum

---

To: Carol Dearing
From: Sarah-Jane MacDonald
Date: December 21, 2022
Subject: Re: Have you got a beard?

I know exactly where last year's beard is. Six feet under, with Joyce's Harry. Don't you remember he had a real white beard? We'll have to get you a new one. I've just added it to the props spreadsheet.

And, Mum, you won't need a dress rehearsal to play Santa. You're on my personnel spreadsheet to babysit Sammy that night. I've booked the Montessori woman for play night, but she's so expensive I need someone to babysit for free during the dress rehearsal. Can Kevin drop Little S around at 5:52 p.m. and collect her when the dress rehearsal is over—whenever that blessed moment may be?

---

To: Sarah-Jane MacDonald
From: Carol Dearing
Date: December 21, 2022
Subject: Re: Have you got a beard?

You know I'll always look after Sammy. Are you sure about the beard? We only ever saw Joyce's Harry at Christmas, so I never knew if the beard was his or not. I'm sure he wasn't allowed out, unless dressed in red with a sack over his shoulder. That reminds me: Have we got a black sack I can put the sweets in? It would look much more authentic if I hand the sweets out from a sack. Let me know. Mum

---

**Message exchange between Sarah-Jane and Kevin MacDonald on December 22, 2022:**

11:21 p.m. Sarah-Jane wrote:
Was Sammy good for Mum? Did she go down ok?

11:30 p.m. Kevin wrote:
Yes, she was awake all day, then flaked out at seven. I've just put her in the car.

11:31 p.m. Sarah-Jane wrote:

Good! Can't wait to see her again after such a stressful dress rehearsal.

11:32 p.m. Kevin wrote:

"Thank you, Kevin, for driving across Lockwood at something-to-midnight, stopping at every red light, after an evening mainlining caffeine in the lighting box."

11:32 p.m. Sarah-Jane wrote:

You know that's what I meant. Hurry home.

11:33 p.m. Sarah-Jane wrote:

When I say "hurry," of course I mean trundle at 10 mph with your nearside wheels in the gutter. Safety first, with children in the car.

11:49 p.m. Kevin wrote:

I'm stopped at the crossing by the church. No one here. Why do people press the button and then, presumably, cross and disappear before it goes green? Everything's quiet. You'd not know we'd been rehearsing here just half an hour ago. Funny thing is, there's a light on in the church hall. I know it was in darkness when I left to pick Sammy up.

11:54 p.m. Sarah-Jane wrote:

The vicar? Checking we switched everything off? I don't know who else would be there.

---

To: The Fairway Players' mailing list
From: Sarah-Jane MacDonald
Date: December 23, 2022
Subject: It's tonight! Oh, yes it is!

Dear all,

So, it's here. *Jack and the Beanstalk*!

Tonight will be the final time we perform this play, and the first time in front of a paying audience. An audience whose ticket money will ensure the church hall roof is fully repaired before next spring's play, *The Hound of the Baskervilles*.

You know your lines, your moves, your backstage jobs, and your role—however small and technically insignificant—in this great hulking machine of a production. Now is the time to engage everything you've learned in the last four weeks and really enjoy the performance—because if we enjoy staging a play, the audience will enjoy watching it. Tomorrow the rehearsal schedule, with all its ups and downs, will be BEHIND YOU and you can enjoy Christmas, secure in the knowledge the church hall roof is a step nearer repair. But tonight you're free to enjoy *this* moment, *your* moment, *Jack's* moment.

Sarah-Jane MacDonald
Director of *Jack and the Beanstalk* and cochair of The Fairway Players

---

To: The Fairway Players' mailing list
From: Celia Halliday
Date: December 23, 2022
Subject: Surprise!

Dear cast and crew of *Jack and the Beanstalk*,
Are *you* in for a treat tonight!

In honor of all your hard work and enthusiasm, the Hallidays—Joel, OBE, Beth, and I—have prepared a huge surprise for the entire group. I won't say anything more than that (else it wouldn't be a surprise), but let's just say you won't believe your eyes when you see it. We don't do things by halves, and this time we've gone all the way. See you tonight!

Celia Halliday
The Fairway Players

---

**Message exchange between Sarah-Jane MacDonald and Celia Halliday on December 23, 2022:**

2:12 p.m. Sarah-Jane wrote:
The Hallidays are key members of this group and I know you only want what's best for it, but an actual play night, with a live audience, isn't the place to spring surprises on cast or crew.

2:15 p.m. Celia wrote:
Let it go, Sarah-Jane. You can't control everything.

---

**Message exchange between Sarah-Jane MacDonald and Carol Dearing on December 23, 2022:**

2:15 p.m. Sarah-Jane wrote:
Bloody Celia! What is she planning? She's trying to take over. I could kill her!

2:17 p.m. Carol wrote:
Get in line, darling. And may I remind you it is more than three weeks since she sent her round-robin.

2:17 p.m. Sarah-Jane wrote:
I haven't had the time!

2:21 p.m. Carol wrote:
If you don't get yours out before Christmas, a fairy will die.

2:29 p.m. Sarah-Jane wrote:
I'm forty-two.

---

**Message exchange between Sarah-Jane and Kevin MacDonald on December 23, 2022:**

2:30 p.m. Sarah-Jane wrote:
Grrr! What do you think this "surprise" is?

2:44 p.m. Kevin wrote:
Odds on: cake. Evens: pizza. Long shot: champagne.

2:50 p.m. Sarah-Jane wrote:
Phew! Of course. You're right. She just wants to wind me up, but I will not be wound. Too much to do, too many people depending on me. Please ask Harley to wait for the sweets and bring them to the hall with the laptop. He ignores my messages.

---

**Message exchange between BKhcCOH94NP and Sarah-Jane MacDonald on December 23, 2022:**

2:56 p.m. BKhcCOH94NP wrote:
Sweets today 5 p.m. COD.

2:57 p.m. Sarah-Jane wrote:
You must be Mick's friend. Hello. Can you confirm exactly what Mick has ordered and the cost, please?

2:58 p.m. BKhcC0H94NP wrote:
Green, white, and brown sweets.

2:59 p.m. Sarah-Jane wrote:
Are they wrapped?

2:59 p.m. BKhcC0H94NP wrote:
Wrapped in eighths and grams.

3:00 p.m. Sarah-Jane wrote:
Fine. And what price did he agree, please?

3:00 p.m. BKhcC0H94NP wrote:
$1900 COD.

3:01 p.m. Sarah-Jane wrote:
$19.00 cash on delivery. Lovely. My son, Harley, will take them in and give you the money.

---

**Message exchange between Sarah-Jane MacDonald and Branded Solutions [Orders] Ltd. on December 23, 2022:**

3:17 p.m. Sarah-Jane wrote:
I've just opened the gift bags you sent. This is not what I ordered.

3:25 p.m. Branded Solutions [Orders] Ltd. wrote:
The order was for fifty gender-neutral Christmas gift bags. What have you received?

3:26 p.m. Sarah-Jane wrote:
Fifty bags, each with the words "gender-neutral" covered in snow and holly.

3:53 p.m. Branded Solutions [Orders] Ltd. wrote:
I've looked it up. Your original order was for bags with "boys" and "girls" lettering, twenty-five each, plus Christmas accents. You changed it on December 9 to the words "gender-neutral" with Christmas accents.

3:54 p.m. Sarah-Jane wrote:
I didn't mean the words. I meant the design.

4:11 p.m. Branded Solutions [Orders] Ltd. wrote:
Oh. It clearly says here "gender-neutral" with Christmas accents. They were delivered last week.

4:13 p.m. Sarah-Jane wrote:
I've been busy and only just opened the box. Oh, for goodness' sake! Well, it's too late to do anything about it now. The children will only be interested in the sweets anyway.

---

**Message exchange between Kevin and Harley MacDonald on December 23, 2022:**

5:18 p.m. Harley wrote:
sweets just arrived, but the guy won't go—he says it's more than $19

5:20 p.m. Kevin wrote:
Well, he told your mother $19. He's trying to pull a fast one, mate. Tell him firmly—with lots of eye contact—that's the price agreed. If he's not happy, he can come to the hall and deal with me.

5:21 p.m. Harley wrote:
he says he's coming to the hall

**Message exchange between Celia Halliday and Sarah-Jane MacDonald on December 23, 2022:**

5:34 p.m. Celia wrote:
Sarah-Jane, are you leaving our audience to freeze outside, or will you open the doors?

5:34 p.m. Sarah-Jane wrote:
We're waiting for Harley to arrive with the laptop, which has all the box-office admin on it. He's on his way with the sweets, which he'll then sort into gift bags. If you still have a "surprise" to deliver to the cast, I suggest you give it out in the greenroom now, so they can eat or drink it and be ready for curtain-up at 6 p.m.

5:35 p.m. Celia wrote:
Our surprise isn't food, Sarah-Jane. And we're "delivering" it onstage tonight. I promise it will bring the house down.

---

**Message exchange between Sarah-Jane MacDonald and Carol Dearing on December 23, 2022:**

5:36 p.m. Sarah-Jane wrote:
I can hear barking. Don't tell me Celia has brought Woof to play night.

5:38 p.m. Carol wrote:
She hasn't. I have. If you want me to dog-sit AND be Santa, something's gotta give. I've brought a bag of chews to keep him quiet.

---

**Message exchange between John O'Dea and Sarah-Jane MacDonald on December 23, 2022:**

5:37 p.m. John wrote:
Fracas at the tea counter. Sign says festive slices eighty-five cents each, three dollars for three. Being interpreted by some audience members as an attempt to commit fraud. Laws are being cited. Adverse publicity threatened. It's a tense standoff between Joyce and a lobby of irate customers.

5:38 p.m. Sarah-Jane wrote:
A standoff over the price of cakes for charity? Why can't they just act their age?

5.38 p.m. John wrote:
They're all aged nine to twelve.

5:39 p.m. Sarah-Jane wrote:
Here's what we'll do. I'll buy the cake slices at the fraudulent price— please give anyone who's complaining a free slice and shut them up.

5:39 p.m. Sarah-Jane wrote:
Ask Kevin for the money later.

---

**Message exchange between Sarah-Jane and Kevin MacDonald on December 23, 2022:**

5:44 p.m. Sarah-Jane wrote:
Thank you for dealing with the sweet man. No need to have taken him out the back. He may be a friend of Mick Payne's, but he wasn't as sketchy as I thought he'd be. In fact, he looked very smart.

5:45 p.m. Kevin wrote:

HE took ME out the back. He wanted $1,900 cash on delivery. When I told him it would have to be paid by credit card, he said it would be $2,500 instead, because it was harder to wash.

5:46 p.m. Sarah-Jane wrote:

$2,500 for a few packets of sweets? That's ridiculous. Mick would never do such a terrible deal. Did you tell him where to stuff his sweets?

5:47 p.m. Kevin wrote:

At first. Then things got heated and I thought it best to pay. He had a wireless card payment machine, FFS.

5:47 p.m. Sarah-Jane wrote:

Where are you? It's curtain-up in thirteen minutes.

5:48 p.m. Kevin wrote:

I'm in a dumpster behind the bathrooms. Can you give me a hand out? Think I've got a black eye.

5:48 p.m. Sarah-Jane wrote:

On my way.

---

**Message exchange between Jade's phone and Sarah-Jane MacDonald on December 23, 2022:**

5:48 p.m. Jade's phone wrote:

Hi, Sarah, me and the kids are outside like you said. Thanks so much for this.

5:48 p.m. Sarah-Jane wrote:

Of course! I'll let you and Aaaliyah in now.

**Message exchange between Elsie Goodwin and Joyce Walford on December 23, 2022:**

5:48 p.m. Elsie wrote:
Joyce, I'm here and sitting down. Is that all I have to do?

5:48 p.m. Joyce wrote:
Did Sarah-Jane look after you?

5:49 p.m. Elsie wrote:
No. I had to find a seat on my own. Where are you, Joyce?

5:50 p.m. Joyce wrote:
At the serving hatch, arguing with our treasurer. Come and get a cup of tea and festive fruit slice before he gives them all away.

5:52 p.m. Elsie wrote:
I can't get up now, in case a child steals my seat. There are a lot of them here. I'm too nervous to eat, Joyce. It would give me a bilious attack.

5:54 p.m. Joyce wrote:
It's a panto in a church hall, Elsie, what's the worst that can happen?

---

**Message exchange between Kevin and Sarah-Jane MacDonald on December 23, 2022:**

5:55 p.m. Kevin wrote:
Where are you? It's a dumpster by the old outside bathroom.

5:55 p.m. Sarah-Jane wrote:
Sorry. I had to let in a poor mother and child, who turned out to be four adults and twelve children. Running back from getting them settled.

5:56 p.m. Kevin wrote:
Where's Harley? Is he ok?

5:56 p.m. Sarah-Jane wrote:
He's fine. He's sorting the sweets into gift bags, ready for distributing at the end.

5:56 p.m. Kevin wrote:
FOR CRYING OUT LOUD! THEY AREN'T SWEETS. THEY'RE DRUGS!

---

**Message exchange between Sarah-Jane MacDonald and Marianne Payne on December 23, 2022:**

5:57 p.m. Sarah-Jane wrote:
Who exactly is the "friend" Mick asked about sweets?

5:58 p.m. Marianne wrote:
He's never told us his name. Between you and me, SJ, he's in with a really bad crowd. But if he can cut a good deal, who cares, eh? Shouldn't you be in the lighting box? The play's due to start in two minutes.

---

**Message exchange between Sarah-Jane and Harley MacDonald on December 23, 2022:**

5:58 p.m. Sarah-Jane wrote:
Harley! Do NOT touch those sweets! Put them out of everyone's reach and don't tell ANYONE ANYTHING.

5:59 p.m. Harley wrote:
fuck's sake what've I done now

5:59 p.m. Sarah-Jane wrote:
Harley, you have not been brought up to swear. Please keep those sweets away from everyone and your mouth SHUT.

5:59 p.m. Harley wrote:
but why

5:59 p.m. Sarah-Jane wrote:
Your dad's accidentally bought some drugs, but I'll sort it out. On my way backstage now with the laptop, then you can concentrate on cueing the music and bringing the house down as Simple Simon.

---

**Message from Jade's phone to Sarah-Jane MacDonald on December 23, 2022:**

5:59 p.m. Jade's phone wrote:
Hope you don't mind, I brought some mums and kids from my childcare group. Really nice of you to put them at the front with all the others. Don't want to gossip, but some have difficult homes. Nice to take them where the kids can be kids for a bit, without any stress or violence. Thanks again.

---

**Message exchange between Myra Briggs and Barry Walford on December 23, 2022:**

5:59 p.m. Myra wrote:
You look sexy as the back end of a cow babes

6:00 p.m. Barry wrote:
ha-ha-ha Nicks got a can of beer down his pants. He bet I can't drink it all before the interval. I bet I can.

6:00 p.m. Myra wrote:

I bet you can love you babes

---

**Messages posted to the Hallidays' WhatsApp group on December 23, 2022:**

**Joel Halliday, OBE**

Are you ready backstage, Beth? Is there enough light? Can you see the trapdoor?

**Beth**

I can just see the catch where you showed me. Yep, ready.

**Celia**

Remember what we said last night.

---

**Message exchange between Emma Crooks and Sarah-Jane MacDonald on December 23, 2022:**

6:02 p.m. Emma wrote:

It's dark backstage and we're all crowded in. Can you ask Kevin to raise the wing lights?

6:02 p.m. Sarah-Jane wrote:

He's busy. Use the lights on your phones.

6:02 p.m. Emma wrote:

Phones aren't allowed backstage.

6:03 p.m. Sarah-Jane wrote:

Well, what are you messaging me on?

---

**Message exchange between Celia Halliday and Sarah-Jane MacDonald on December 23, 2022:**

6:05 p.m. Celia wrote:

What's the delay, Sarah-Jane? We're all in position and ready to go.

6:05 p.m. Sarah-Jane wrote:

Kevin was held up. He's back in the lighting box now. He'll set up the program and sneak down for the crowd scenes. Everything's fine.

6:06 p.m. Celia wrote:

Good. Because our surprise happens soon after the opening number. Make sure you're in the audience to see it.

6:07 p.m. Sarah-Jane wrote:

Yes, yes. Apart from the crowd scenes. I'll nip through the kitchen for those. I'm about to cue lights, music, and curtains. Let the pantomime commence!

---

**Message from Jade's phone to Sarah-Jane MacDonald on December 23, 2022:**

6:12 p.m. Jade's phone wrote:
Wow! What a spectacular start. We love that song. I had such a crush on Pharrell as a kid. And the line about the room without a roof totally fits, with the actual hole in the roof. Brilliant! Did you know there's a hole in the beanstalk, too?

---

**Message exchange between Sarah-Jane MacDonald and Emma Crooks on December 23, 2022:**

6:13 p.m. Sarah-Jane wrote:
Emma, I'm outside looking in at the window, so can't do anything at the moment, but next time you're onstage please can you reassure me there's no hole in the beanstalk.

6:13 p.m. Emma wrote:
How did you know my phone was still on?

6:14 p.m. Sarah-Jane wrote:
It's shining through your pocket like a billboard for Samsung. Please inspect the beanstalk, let me know, and then switch it OFF.

6:14 p.m. Emma wrote:
Why are you watching from outside? Shouldn't you be in the lighting box with Kevin?

6:14 p.m. Sarah-Jane wrote:
Please, please, please, Emma—the beanstalk . . .

**Message exchange between Fran Elroy-Jones and Dustin Perez on December 23, 2022:**

6:19 p.m. Fran wrote:
The young boy doing the music seems distracted. I hope he cues all the tracks properly and gets out onstage in time to say his lines.

6:23 p.m. Dustin wrote:
He's stashed the sweets in the knotted hanky he carries as Simple Simon and is hauling them onstage tied to a stick. I haven't been able to nab so much as a Gobstopper!

---

**Message exchange between Sarah-Jane and Kevin MacDonald on December 23, 2022:**

6:14 p.m. Sarah-Jane wrote:
Kevin! There are five dumpsters. Make a noise, so I know which one to open.

6:14 p.m. Sarah-Jane wrote:
Which dumpster are you in?

6:15 p.m. Sarah-Jane wrote:
I know it took me a while to get here, but surely you haven't gone to sleep? You're supposed to be playing the Giant in forty-seven pages' time. Don't tell me that's something else I have to do!

---

**Message exchange between Emma Crooks and Sarah-Jane MacDonald on December 23, 2022:**

6:24 p.m. Emma wrote:
The beanstalk's fine. I took care of it.

6:24 p.m. Sarah-Jane wrote:
Wonderful! That's just what I need to hear. What was wrong?

6:25 p.m. Emma wrote:
There's a little window in the trunk. It was unlatched. When the lights were down, I jammed it shut. There's no way it'll open now.

6:25 p.m. Sarah-Jane wrote:
You're a star! Thank you, Emma.

6:25 p.m. Emma wrote:
No problem. It's going well, isn't it?

6:26 p.m. Sarah-Jane wrote:
Emma. Your phone. Off. Switch. Please.

---

**Message exchange between Sarah-Jane MacDonald and Carol Dearing on December 23, 2022:**

6:28 p.m. Sarah-Jane wrote:
Mum, I'm dealing with something outside by the dumpsters. Why has everything gone quiet in the hall?

6:28 p.m. Carol wrote:

The Fairy Godmother is supposed to scoot on, but Beth is nowhere to be found. Emma is loitering onstage like a lemon with a very wobbly Daisy the Cow. Cast and audience alike are waiting with bated breath.

6:29 p.m. Sarah-Jane wrote:

For goodness' sake, where's Beth?

6:29 p.m. Carol wrote:

I don't want to tell tales, but Emma has her mobile phone in the back pocket of her lederhosen. Is the beanstalk haunted?

6:30 p.m. Sarah-Jane wrote:

Don't be ridiculous! Of course it isn't haunted.

6:30 p.m. Carol wrote:

Well, there are some unholy thuds and groans coming from it. Where are you?

6:31 p.m. Sarah-Jane wrote:

Trying to get this bloody dumpster open. The audience laughed just then. Things must be back on track.

6:31 p.m. Carol wrote:

Sadly, no. They're laughing because Emma got a notification from John Lewis.

---

**Message posted to the Hallidays' WhatsApp group on December 23, 2022:**

**Joel Halliday, OBE**

Beth—what are you waiting for? Now—GO!

**Message exchange between Elsie Goodwin and Joyce Walford on December 23, 2022:**

6:32 p.m. Elsie wrote:
Was that meant to happen, Joyce?

6:34 p.m. Joyce wrote:
During rehearsals she rode in on one of those electric scooters. They might've changed it. No one tells me anything, Elsie.

---

**Message from the Rev. Joshua Harries to Sarah-Jane MacDonald on December 23, 2022:**

6:32 p.m. Rev. Joshua Harries wrote:
My goodness, Sarah-Jane! Mother and I heard that scream in the vicarage. The panto must be going down a storm. Bravo to The Fairway Players!

---

## *The Lockwood Gazette* online feature, December 24, 2022:

### IS THAT A DEAD BODY IN THE BEANSTALK? OH, YES IT IS!

**Femi**
Well, that came out of the long grass.

**Charlotte**
A body? I thought this was about an accidental drugs deal.

**Femi**
The Hallidays were planning a surprise that involved the beanstalk and their daughter, Beth. Was she sealed inside when Emma closed the trapdoor? She could have suffocated.

**Charlotte**
A Christmas tragedy. Surely, as committed Fairway Players, Celia, Joel, and Beth would never do anything that seriously jeopardized the performance? Or would they—if it meant Sarah-Jane was ousted as chair?

**Femi**
Sarah-Jane knows the Hallidays resent her, but allows them to produce one play a year.

**Charlotte**
On December 1 she said she wants their tenure to be based on "hard work, clear heads, and a sense of fairness."

**Femi**

Or is she just keeping her enemies close? Celia is delighted to hear about the asbestos scandal.

**Charlotte**

A body in the beanstalk. Yet Mr. Tanner has only given us the headline, not the newspaper article itself. He must want our response to the material so far.

**Femi**

Who are the mysterious Dexters? They auditioned, were cast, then never showed up to rehearsals again?

**Charlotte**

When Sarah-Jane snooped around their house she found it deserted, and mail piled up on the mat. Could the body be one of them?

**Femi**

If there's a drugs gang in the area, then the body could be entirely unconnected to The Fairway Players.

**Charlotte**

True. The beanstalk has been in storage with the Fowey Light Operatic Society and used by other local groups over the years. We don't know how long the body has been there.

**Femi**
Who was in the church hall when Kevin drove Sammy back from Carol's late at night after the dress rehearsal?

**Charlotte**
I can't help suspecting Celia of *something*—the way she checked with John that they aren't covered by insurance, if they have to refund ticket money.

**Femi**
We need more to go on. Let's collaborate on an email to Mr. Tanner.

To: Roderick Tanner, KC
From: Femi Hassan & Charlotte Holroyd
Date: November 5, 2023
Subject: Re: A conundrum for you


Dear Mr. Tanner,

Thank you for this intriguing bundle of documents. Charlotte and I have been feverishly reading. We've isolated several key areas of interest, which may have a bearing on what we take to be a murder case. They are as follows:

1. The Fairway Players now have two competing couples who vie for the coveted position of committee chairs: the MacDonalds and the Hallidays.
2. The MacDonalds, as elected leaders, do not have the unquestioning support enjoyed by group founders the Haywards. Some members resent not being given roles, and happily challenge Sarah-Jane in a way we remember they did not when Martin was chair. Would they collude to undermine Sarah-Jane's leadership with the type of scandal that would cancel a performance?
3. There are new housing projects popping up around Lockwood, which means a flurry of outsiders. This could spark tensions with the established locals, but more than this—the anonymity of a newly expanding community could unwittingly shelter more ruthless criminal gangs.
4. New member Dustin Perez overheard talk that a convicted murderer was in the area. Peter Halliday, the son Celia and

Joel never speak about, is known to have been in trouble with the law. Why was he imprisoned, and could he have been released?

We very much hope to have alighted upon something relevant with these points—and look forward to receiving more evidence in due course.

Yours sincerely,
Femi Hassan and Charlotte Holroyd

---

To: Femi Hassan & Charlotte Holroyd
From: Roderick Tanner, KC
Date: November 5, 2023
Subject: Re: A conundrum for you

Dear both,

You may be correct—that this is a murder case. I'm sending you further correspondence. Can you tell me who the victim is?

RT
Roderick Tanner, KC (retired)

---

**Femi**

Mr. Tanner's original email clearly states that The Fairway Players are at the center of this mystery. To me that suggests both victim and perpetrator are members of the group. Who might be the victim?

> **Charlotte**
>
> Kevin has a run-in with a drug dealer just prior to curtain-up.

**Femi**

Sarah-Jane is (secretly) letting a poor family see the show for free and is sidetracked when she has to sneak them in, then Jade spots a "hole" in the beanstalk. By the time she gets outside, there is no answer from Kevin.

> **Charlotte**
>
> She wonders if he's fallen asleep. But he could have lost consciousness. Suffocated in the dumpster?

**Femi**

Was he ever in a dumpster? Or does someone else steal his phone and pretend to be him, with texts that lure Sarah-Jane outside? Someone who knows Kevin and how he communicates.

**Charlotte**
They'd have to know about the drugs, too. Surely not Harley? If Kevin's dead, how does his body get inside the beanstalk?

**Femi**
How does ANYONE'S body get inside a beanstalk?

# County Police Interview Report

Extract from police interview with Beth Halliday, December 24, 2022:

**Sgt. Crowe:** So, you were dressed up as the Fairy Godmother and waiting backstage. What happened next?

**Ms. Halliday:** I handed my electric scooter to one of the other actors. I didn't need it.

**Sgt. Crowe:** Because you had wings?

**Ms. Halliday:** Because Dad wanted the Fairy Godmother to appear from inside the beanstalk. The wings were just lace and wire.

**Sgt. Crowe:** Of course. Why the last-minute change to what had been rehearsed?

**Ms. Halliday:** Mum and Dad thought it would be a nice surprise if the Fairy Godmother popped out of the beanstalk. We only rehearsed it last night. It was no big deal.

**Sgt. Crowe:** This trapdoor. How did your parents know it was there?

**Ms. Halliday:** They remembered from the last time The Fairway Players did *Jack and the Beanstalk*. Back in the day.

**Sgt. Crowe:** I understand the trapdoor had been sealed up. Why was that?

**Ms. Halliday:** I don't know. But Dad got it open. He found the screws and chiseled the filler out. It's concealed in the trunk. You can't see it when it's closed.

**Sgt. Crowe:** Were you there when he opened the trapdoor for the first time?

**Ms. Halliday:** Yes. It was after dress rehearsal, when everyone else had left.

**Sgt. Crowe:** And was that when you got inside the beanstalk for the first time?

**Ms. Halliday:** No, I didn't bother. We peered in, and it was obviously big enough. It was late, so we just ran through what I should do when it was my time to appear.

**Sgt. Crowe:** And what was that?

**Ms. Halliday:** Well, they wanted me to pop my head out of the trapdoor and say my lines from there. As a surprise for the cast.

**Sgt. Crowe:** You're twenty years old, Ms. Halliday. Do you do everything your parents tell you? Even when it might disrupt the play for your fellow actors, some of whom have never been onstage before and need the performance to go exactly as it did at rehearsals?

**Ms. Halliday:** I know what you're saying. It's just they've put up with a lot lately. My brother was released from prison earlier this year and they won't have him back. I've dropped out of university, but they still threw a big surprise party for me. I wish they hadn't, but what can you say? I mean, I used to love The Saturdays when I was a kid . . . I'm into grime now. Dad's business has slumped, but they constantly tell people everything's going well. I simply wanted to keep them happy.

**Sgt. Crowe:** So, on the night, you went along with their— potentially disruptive—surprise.

**Ms. Halliday:** Yes.

**Sgt. Crowe:** Can we go back to the previous evening, when you and your parents peered into the cavity revealed by the newly opened trapdoor. Can you tell me what was in there?

**Ms. Halliday:** It was musty and airless. Obviously hadn't been opened for years. The base was rock-solid with polystyrene filler. Dad said if it was suddenly released, it would expand instantly and burst out in a torrent.

**Sgt. Crowe:** So you were careful . . .

**Ms. Halliday:** In the blackout before the play started, I climbed in through the trapdoor. I left it unlatched and slightly open, so I could still hear my cue.

**Sgt. Crowe:** No one saw you climb in?

**Ms. Halliday:** They were all getting in place for the opening number. "Happy" by Pharrell.

**Sgt. Crowe:** A solid toe tapper.

**Ms. Halliday:** Only the lighting wasn't right. The blackout afterward lasted too long. At some point someone latched the door back up. I heard my cue line and pushed the trapdoor, but it was jammed shut. I had to get it open, so I gave it a kick, then another and another . . .

**Sgt. Crowe:** One eyewitness says, "The entire beanstalk split in two down the middle and the Fairy Godmother surfed out on an ever-expanding wave of polystyrene curls."

**Ms. Halliday:** That's about it, yep.

**Sgt. Crowe:** Only polystyrene curls weren't all that was inside the beanstalk.

**Ms. Halliday:** No. I came to a stop at the front of the stage, and although I was a bit dazed, I quickly realized something else had . . . surfed out with me.

**Sgt. Crowe:** A dead body.

**Ms. Halliday:** Uh-huh.

**Sgt. Crowe:** A dead body in a Santa suit.

**Message exchange between Sarah-Jane and Harley MacDonald on December 23, 2022:**

6:32 p.m. Sarah-Jane wrote:
What was that? They shouldn't be screaming now. The play has only just started.

6:32 p.m. Harley wrote:
if you're in the lighting box with dad you must be able to see it

6:33 p.m. Sarah-Jane wrote:
I'm in the backyard, helping Dad out of a dumpster. It's not the work of a moment.

6:33 p.m. Harley wrote:
jack and the beanstalk just got really dark

6:33 p.m. Sarah-Jane wrote:
Find Grandma. She'll sort out any problem. Remember she's dressed as Santa.

## *County Police Interview Report*

Extract from police interview with Denise Malcolm, December 24, 2022:

**Sgt. Crowe:** Thanks for coming in, Mrs. Malcolm.

**Mrs. Malcolm:** What's this about?

**Sgt. Crowe:** The body in the beanstalk. Is there anything else I should be speaking to The Fairway Players about?

**Mrs. Malcolm:** Not that I know of.

**Sgt. Crowe:** How long have you been a member of the group, Denise?

**Mrs. Malcolm:** Since it began. Eighty-four, eighty-five. More than thirty-five years.

**Sgt. Crowe:** But you're a backstage member, looking after costumes, makeup . . . you've never fancied treading the boards?

**Mrs. Malcolm:** I audition for every play. I've had a couple of walk-on parts.

**Sgt. Crowe:** But you never seem to get a meaty role, do you? Is that a problem?

**Mrs. Malcolm:** Not for long. I'm playing the female lead in *The Hound of the Baskervilles* next spring. Celia said I'm perfect for it.

**Sgt. Crowe:** Which version? If it's the one I saw in the West End recently, the only woman in it is a housekeeper, who has two lines at most, spoken from the wings. It's one of those modern comedies.

**Mrs. Malcolm:** What . . . ? But . . .

**Sgt. Crowe:** For the benefit of the transcript, Mrs. Malcolm is lost for words.

**Mrs. Malcolm:** I'm *not* lost for words, Sergeant. I've got so much to say, I don't know what to say first! Celia *promised*! She promised me a leading role. Do you know something?

**Sgt. Crowe:** Er . . .

**Mrs. Malcolm:** When we did *An Evening with Gary Lineker* the roof collapsed and we had to postpone. The chap playing Lineker was on vacation for the new dates and there was a hue and cry to find a replacement. I put myself forward, and who do the MacDonalds choose instead? Joyce Walford. She's sixty-seven.

**Sgt. Crowe:** And you are . . . ?

**Mrs. Malcolm:** Sixty-four.

**Sgt. Crowe:** You were angry about that?

**Mrs. Malcolm:** I'm *still* fuming!

**Sgt. Crowe:** Enough to sabotage the MacDonalds' pantomime?

**Mrs. Malcolm:** I'm a Fairway Player, Sergeant. I'd never spoil a play, not for anything or anyone. But there's something you should know: the Hallidays were planning something. Not the surprise they told us about afterward—Beth saying her lines from the trapdoor—something else. Although I'll be honest, even now I can't tell you if their plan went wrong or *right*.

**Sgt. Crowe:** Can you elaborate?

**Mrs. Malcolm:** Well, I told Celia the beanstalk is made of asbestos. She told me to keep quiet about it.

**Sgt. Crowe:** Understandably. That news would jeopardize the production. Why did you agree, when you must know asbestos is dangerous?

**Mrs. Malcolm:** Because of the role she promised me in *The Hound of the Baskervilles*. She didn't want anyone looking at that beanstalk too closely. It was all part of their plan.

**Sgt. Crowe:** Hmmm . . . it's very interesting. The asbestos rumors that surround this beanstalk. I suspect they are what led to the trapdoor being screwed shut, and whenever that happened, the body was sealed inside. You see the connection?

**Mrs. Malcolm:** Whatever it is, I'm *certain* it was the Hallidays.

**Sgt. Crowe:** *You* told Celia the beanstalk was made of asbestos, Denise, but who told you?

**Mrs. Malcolm:** Dunno. Soon as I saw that old thing I remembered talk of it, back in the old days. Joyce and Marianne were there. They may remember. Have you found out who the body was?

**Sgt. Crowe:** I can't divulge such information at this stage, I'm afraid.

**Mrs. Malcolm:** Have you spoken to the Hallidays' son Peter? A proper roughie. Always in trouble. He disappeared a few years ago. They said he went traveling. Turns out, only as far as HMP Brackwell.

**Sgt. Crowe:** He's in prison? What for?

**Mrs. Malcolm:** Drugs and violence, or so I heard. But what if that wasn't all he did? What if he killed someone, and the Hallidays hid the body in the beanstalk so he didn't get life?

Joel knows all the local groups. They swap props and scenery all the time. Wouldn't be difficult for him to track down that beanstalk and hide a body in it. Imagine how they must've felt when it turned up onstage in the middle of the annual panto. For the benefit of the transcript, Sergeant Crowe takes a deep breath.

**Sgt. Crowe:** It's not necessary for you to narrate for me, Denise. What makes you think the Hallidays were plotting anything?

**Mrs. Malcolm:** After dress rehearsal on Thursday, I was walking my dog. It was eleven-thirty, a good half hour after we'd left the church hall. But I saw the light was still on. I crept up to the window and peered in, worried it was left on accidentally. But it wasn't.

**Sgt. Crowe:** What did you see?

**Mrs. Malcolm:** The Hallidays. Joel, Celia, and Beth, all stood around the beanstalk. It was only when I saw that body in the middle of the stage, in the middle of the pantomime, that I realized why she told me to keep quiet. She must've known the body was there.

**Message exchange between Carol Dearing and Sarah-Jane MacDonald on December 23, 2022:**

6:34 p.m. Carol wrote:
Where are you? Hell's breaking loose.

6:34 p.m. Sarah-Jane MacDonald wrote:
Whatever it is, can you take care of it, please, Mum? I'm busy at the moment.

6:34 p.m. Carol wrote:
You're not as busy as we are backstage, I can assure you.

6:35 p.m. Sarah-Jane MacDonald wrote:
Kevin's covered in dumpster juice. I'm getting him into clothes from the props box. Nothing fits. What's happening down there? I can hear laughter and applause, so it can't be that bad.

6:36 p.m. Carol wrote:
The beanstalk split in two. The Fairy Godmother and a skeleton dressed as Father Christmas slid out at a fair speed. They hit Daisy the Cow, who also split in two. The front half emitted a fountain of lager. The two halves are rolling around the stage now, covered in beer, trying to get up. We're all trying to help, but we keep slipping on polystyrene curls and cheap lager. The skeleton is seated in the midst of it all, like King Canute in the waves.

# County Police Interview Report

Extract from police interview with Celia Halliday, December 24, 2022:

**Sgt. Crowe:** So, can you explain *exactly* what your plan was?

**Mrs. Halliday:** No comment.

**Sgt. Crowe:** You're not under arrest, Mrs. Halliday. You're a witness, no more.

**Mrs. Halliday:** No comment.

**Sgt. Crowe:** That wasn't even a question.

**Mrs. Halliday:** No comment.

**Sgt. Crowe:** This is an unexplained death that *may* turn into a murder case, depending on the results of the autopsy.

**Mrs. Halliday:** No comment.

**Sgt. Crowe:** You and your husband, Joel Halliday, arranged for . . .

**Mrs. Halliday:** Joel Halliday, OBE.

**Sgt. Crowe:** Together you arranged for your daughter to spring out of the beanstalk during one of the early scenes in *Jack and the Beanstalk*. Why was this a complete surprise to everyone else in the cast, when the play had been in rehearsal for four weeks?

**Mrs. Halliday:** No comment.

**Sgt. Crowe:** Why sabotage a fundraiser for the church hall, where you intend to stage *The Hound of the Baskervilles* next spring?

**Mrs. Halliday:** No comment. Except to say . . . oh, I don't know. Bloody Sarah-Jane.

**Sgt. Crowe:** Sarah-Jane MacDonald, cochair of The Fairway Players and director of the pantomime?

**Mrs. Halliday:** She's so bloody perfect. Everything she does, however small, blossoms into a huge success. She's touched by magic. We just wanted *Jack and the Beanstalk* to go down in Fairways' history as the most disastrous production ever.

**Sgt. Crowe:** I remember The Fairway Players were involved in another murder case a few years ago. A nurse was pushed from a balcony. Surely that was the most disastrous production ever?

**Mrs. Halliday:** Not at all. *All My Sons* was very well received by press and public alike.

**Sgt. Crowe:** Well, it's my understanding the cast and crew of *Jack and the Beanstalk* carried on with the production, despite the dead body that, er, appeared onstage. Apparently, many audience members praised the unexpected plot turns and said it appealed to their children more than ordinary pantos.

**Mrs. Halliday:** There you are! Everything goes right in the end for bloody Sarah-Jane.

**Sgt. Crowe:** The grass is always greener. Other people's lives often seem better than our own—because usually we don't get to see inside the beanstalk.

**Mrs. Halliday:** You said "another murder." Earlier. The Fairway Players were involved in "another murder case a few years ago." You must suspect this death is a murder, too.

**Sgt. Crowe:** Do you, Mrs. Halliday? Do you suspect this death is a murder, too?

**Mrs. Halliday:** No comment.

**Message from Jade's phone to Sarah-Jane MacDonald on December 23, 2022:**

6:35 p.m. Jade's phone wrote:
Best panto ever! Never laughed so much in my life, and the kids are loving it. Thanks for letting us in xxxx

---

**Message exchange between Elsie Goodwin and Joyce Walford on December 23, 2022:**

6:38 p.m. Elsie Goodwin wrote:
I'd have brought my neighbor (who plays flugel in an orchestra) if I'd known it was one of those arty performances where it's all modern dance and no one speaks.

6:38 p.m. Joyce wrote:
Can't reply, Elsie. Backstage. Got to help my Nick and Barry sort things out.

6:41 p.m. Elsie Goodwin wrote:
There's a lady Santa has run on. Your boys are helping her put the skeleton in the Sainsbury's cart. They're wet through with beer, but they're ok.

6:43 p.m. Joyce wrote:
I can't text, Elsie. I got to make sure.

6:43 p.m. Elsie wrote:
Dame Trot said something about the beanstalk being deadly. She must mean climate change. The skeleton represents mankind. It's all gone woke, Joyce.

## *County Police Interview Report*

Extract from police interview with Joel Halliday, December 24, 2022:

**Sgt. Crowe:** Joel Halliday. Can you explain what your role is at The Fairway Players?

**Mr. Halliday:** I can. I've been a member since the group was founded in the mid-1980s. I'm on the committee because I plan and organize our sets and scenery. In *Jack and the Beanstalk* I was cast as Dame Trot.

**Sgt. Crowe:** The pantomime dame.

**Mr. Halliday:** Yes.

**Sgt. Crowe:** That must have been fun.

**Mr. Halliday:** It was.

**Sgt. Crowe:** After the dress rehearsal on Thursday night, I understand you, your wife, and daughter stayed behind, even though everyone else had left.

**Mr. Halliday:** We did. My backstage role involves securing the set and tidying away props. We're always last to leave.

**Sgt. Crowe:** Only I understand you had an agenda on this particular night.

**Mr. Halliday:** It was all a joke. We just wanted to mess with them.

**Sgt. Crowe:** Who?

**Mr. Halliday:** The MacDonalds. They take themselves far too seriously. The Fairway Players' annual panto has always been a rough-and-ready fundraiser. A few rehearsals, improvised script, minimal set building. Who wants the worry of staging a polished production, with all the work that entails, at a time of year when we're all so busy? No one. We always had a great time and the kids used to love it. Until the MacDonalds barged their way to joint chairs. Suddenly we're rehearsing four days a week, learning dance routines and sourcing West End scenery. Authenticity of the script? It's a panto from the seventies, for goodness' sake!

**Sgt. Crowe:** So you planned a joke that would . . . what? Because the Fairy Godmother saying her lines from the trapdoor, instead of a scooter, isn't going to cause too much of a problem, is it?

**Mr. Halliday:** We didn't know . . .

**Sgt. Crowe:** You knew it could split in two. The beanstalk is constructed from two halves. The trapdoor is set in the join. It's a weak spot in the design that may have led to it being sealed up at some point. Only the night before the play, you reopened that weak spot. To the point that all it took was someone giving the trapdoor a good kicking and the whole structure would come apart, releasing whatever it contained onto the stage. Why?

**Mr. Halliday:** Just . . . Sarah-Jane . . .

**Sgt. Crowe:** Do you object to Sarah-Jane being in charge?

**Mr. Halliday:** No . . .

**Sgt. Crowe:** But you do. There's something about her being in control that makes you want to take her down. What is that?

**Mr. Halliday:** It's nothing, but . . . Celia and I were second-in-command to Martin and Helen Hayward. Sarah-Jane and Kevin, well, they only knew the Haywards through Sarah-Jane's mother, Carol.

**Sgt. Crowe:** The MacDonalds were *elected* cochairs. Voted for democratically by the group.

**Mr. Halliday:** I'm sure there was some underhand lobbying, or something . . .

**Sgt. Crowe:** Perhaps your grudge is not only with Sarah-Jane, but with The Fairway Players themselves. You wanted to see the group in chaos. The group who didn't want you or your family at the helm.

**Mr. Halliday:** Who says I have a grudge?

**Sgt. Crowe:** For the benefit of the transcript, Mr. Halliday has taken and is holding a folded sheet of paper I've just given him. It was found in Dame Trot's apron, which officers discovered discarded on the stage.

### *A hastily handwritten paragraph*
### *on a sheet of paper, folded six times:*

Oh no, boys and girls! Our magical beanstalk has broken apart. This is terrible news for everyone in Cloud Land and Lockwood. The beanstalk is made from asbestos and its dust is deadly. I'm afraid I have to stop this performance immediately and ask that the audience leave as quickly and quietly as possible by the rear doors. Please see our director, Sarah-Jane MacDonald, about refunding your ticket money.

## *County Police Interview Report*

Further extract from police interview with Joel Halliday, December 24, 2022:

**Sgt. Crowe:** Have you read it?

**Mr. Halliday:** Yes.

**Sgt. Crowe:** These lines aren't in the script. You wrote them for Dame Trot, the character you play.

**Mr. Halliday:** Yes.

**Sgt. Crowe:** They are for when Beth looks out through the trapdoor and the beanstalk cracks through that carefully orchestrated fault line. For when you step forward, like a hero, to stop the play and save cast and audience alike from inhaling asbestos dust.

**Mr. Halliday:** Surely you can see the sense in that.

**Sgt. Crowe:** But you didn't say the lines you'd prepared. Why not?

**Mr. Halliday:** I started to say them, but rushed to help Beth, too concerned about her to . . . So the show went on.

**Sgt. Crowe:** Because things didn't go totally to plan. For the benefit of the transcript, Mr. Halliday is staring at his hands.

**Mr. Halliday:** It was only meant to fall gently apart. Just enough to worry everyone.

**Sgt. Crowe:** Only Beth couldn't open the trapdoor. Someone had closed the latch. She was locked inside, understandably she panicked and tried to kick it open with increasing force. A force that . . . rent the beanstalk violently asunder.

**Mr. Halliday:** If you want to be Shakespearean about it.

**Sgt. Crowe:** When did you hear rumors the beanstalk was made of asbestos?

**Mr. Halliday:** A few days ago. Denise Malcolm told my wife.

**Sgt. Crowe:** And how did Denise know?

**Mr. Halliday:** Well, she's been a member as long as we have, so . . . I'm not sure. She must remember talk about asbestos last time it was here.

**Sgt. Crowe:** Something puzzles me, Mr. Halliday. You heard the beanstalk could contain a potentially deadly substance, released as dust when the material is broken up.

**Mr. Halliday:** Yes.

**Sgt. Crowe:** Yet you happily exposed Beth to it. For the benefit of the transcript, Mr. Halliday is looking sheepish. Let me take you back to the previous night, after dress rehearsal. With your wife and beloved daughter standing by, you released the screws holding the two halves together and gently chiseled the trapdoor open. Having done so, you all peered gingerly inside, careful not to disturb the beanstalk's now-delicate structure, to a dusty cavity that hadn't been opened in years, and stood around talking about the plan.

**Mr. Halliday:** Yes.

**Sgt. Crowe:** Why would you do that? Risk the health of your wife and child—as well as your own—even if the asbestos was just a rumor. Most people would happily not take that small chance. I see you're lost for words, so I'll continue. Mr. Halliday, I suspect you happily exposed your family to the beanstalk because you know very well it contains not a scrap of asbestos. You know it's made from a water-based fibrous resin that is common in professional stage scenery. It's perfectly safe, whether broken apart or not. The plan was to create an asbestos scare, stop the performance, and suggest the audience claim their ticket money back, thus minimizing the funds raised by the play and rendering it the least-successful production the group has ever staged. The plan is completely and utterly malicious in intent and execution.

**Mr. Halliday:** It was a joke! A fire for Sarah-Jane to put out. It's not illegal, so I don't know why you're even speaking to me and my family.

**Sgt. Crowe:** You're here because the beanstalk contained a very well-hidden dead body. Did you know about that?

**Mr. Halliday:** You think I'd allow Beth anywhere near a corpse? No way. No way on earth.

**Sgt. Crowe:** Your son Peter. He was in prison for drug dealing and ABH.

**Mr. Halliday:** He's out now. But we haven't seen him. He's not welcome at our home.

**Sgt. Crowe:** If you knew your son had killed someone, Mr. Halliday, would you hide the body, perhaps in a large stage prop, so that he was only convicted of much lesser charges? Then, perhaps, create the impression he wasn't welcome at your home?

**Mr. Halliday:** Absolutely not. If I knew my son had killed someone, I'd march him to the nearest police station myself. That body was a skeleton!

**Sgt. Crowe:** A mummified skeleton . . .

**Mr. Halliday:** Whatever it was—*whoever* it was—has been dead for *years*. Peter would've been a child. This is ridiculous. I'm going home.

**Message exchange between Myra Briggs and Barry Walford on December 23, 2022:**

6:43 p.m. Myra wrote:
u ok babe look like u pissed urself wiv beer

6:43 p.m. Barry wrote:
Love you, babe. Remember that, yeah?

---

**Message exchange between Kevin MacDonald and Sarah-Jane MacDonald on December 23, 2022:**

6:51 p.m. Kevin wrote:
Whatever it is can't be as bad as what just happened to me, for God's sake! I was assaulted by a criminal kingpin and left for dead!

6:51 p.m. Sarah-Jane wrote:
It's much worse than that. Get your cape on and come to the stage immediately.

6:52 p.m. Kevin wrote:
Where are the drugs?

6:52 p.m. Sarah-Jane wrote:
SWEETS! The SWEETS are safe with Harley. They're the least of our worries.

6:53 p.m. Kevin wrote:
Why do you need me? I'm not on till the end.

6:53 p.m. Sarah-Jane wrote:
We've laid the skeleton on the wall panel and have balanced it on Simple Simon's Sainsbury's cart to whisk it out of the hall as quickly as possible.

6:53 p.m. Kevin wrote:

On my way. What skeleton?

6:54 p.m. Sarah-Jane wrote:

That is a question for after the play. We'll have to wheel it down the aisle, but I'm sure we can make it entertaining for the children—jokes, banter, etc., as we go.

6:54 p.m. Kevin wrote:

Really? We don't want to make a bad situation worse.

6:54 p.m. Sarah-Jane wrote:

How could this possibly be any worse?

6:55 p.m. Kevin wrote:

Didn't Father Josh expressly tell us to take care of that wall panel?

---

### The *Lockwood Gazette* online feature, December 24, 2022:

#### IS THAT A DEAD BODY IN THE BEANSTALK? OH, YES IT IS!

*Kids "delighted" as mummified skeleton paraded through church hall on SAINSBURY'S cart with "Live well for less at Christmas" on front. Dog follows "with leg bone."*

---

**Message exchange between Kevin MacDonald and Sarah-Jane MacDonald on December 23, 2022:**

6:55 p.m. Kevin wrote:
Woof has just run past me. I've gone wobbly, SJ. I've had to sit down in the foyer. He has a leg bone in his mouth. A bone from a skeleton.

6:57 p.m. Sarah-Jane wrote:
For goodness' sake! Of course he hasn't. You know I'm a perfectionist—I have the ENTIRE skeleton here. Woof has a DOG CHEW shaped like a bone. Please find a helmet and truncheon to match the cape. The audience will appreciate the reassurance of a policeman on the premises.

---

**Message from Jade's phone to Sarah-Jane MacDonald on December 23, 2022:**

6:59 p.m. Jade's phone wrote:
Ha-ha! Aaaliyah says can he ride on the flying carpet with Halloween Santa and his dog? Brilliant.

---

**Message exchange between Carol Dearing and Sarah-Jane MacDonald on December 23, 2022:**

7:01 p.m. Carol wrote:
What is Kevin wearing? Have you not done your ironing?

7:01 p.m. Sarah-Jane wrote:
It's a Victorian police uniform from the props box. Do you know where Woof is?

7:01 p.m. Carol wrote:

He was here before all that kerfuffle.

7:02 p.m. Sarah-Jane wrote:

Well, now he's up in the lighting box with me, gnawing on a bone-shaped chew.

7:02 p.m. Carol wrote:

He doesn't have a bone-shaped chew.

7:03 p.m. Sarah-Jane wrote:

Shit! Mum, please rally everyone backstage and return to the script. They can work around the collapsed beanstalk. Congratulate Harley and Fran for improvising while the rest of us cleaned up. The show must go on . . .

# County Police Interview Report

Extract from police interview with Marianne Payne, December 24, 2022:

**Sgt. Crowe:** You're not under arrest, Mrs. Payne, we're just trying to ascertain whose body was hidden in the beanstalk and how they came to be there.

**Mrs. Payne:** I've never seen him before in my life, Officer.

**Sgt. Crowe:** Well, his closest friends wouldn't recognize him now, but he was dressed as Santa Claus when he died. That should tell us something.

**Mrs. Payne:** That he fell down a chimney?

**Sgt. Crowe:** Perhaps. But how did his body find its way into a pantomime beanstalk, and who then covered him with polystyrene filler? Because whoever did that also stamped down that filler until it was completely impacted, sealed the trapdoor and then, quite possibly, started rumors that it contained asbestos, to stop anyone opening it up ever again.

**Mrs. Payne:** Never thought of it like that, Officer. You're right. Frightening. Who'd kill Father Christmas? The world's gone mad.

**Sgt. Crowe:** It went mad a long time ago, Mrs. Payne. Thirty years, to be precise. The exact same time this beanstalk was last used by The Fairway Players.

**Message exchange between Sarah-Jane MacDonald and Kevin MacDonald on December 23, 2022:**

7:11 p.m. Sarah-Jane wrote:
The skeleton is safely stashed in the cloakroom cupboard, its shinbone wrestled from Woof, who is back in the greenroom with a pig's ear. The polystyrene filler is swept away and the beer mopped up. We're back on-script. Stay in the box and cue the lights.

7:11 p.m. Kevin wrote:
Shall I come down and fill in a couple of crowd scenes?

7:12 p.m. Sarah-Jane wrote:
No. For heaven's sake, stay in the lighting box and do your job.

7:13 p.m. Kevin wrote:
Thank you, Kevin, for coming back from the dead and saving the play.

7:13 p.m. Sarah-Jane wrote:
You know that's what I meant.

---

**Message exchange between Carol Dearing and Sarah-Jane MacDonald on December 23, 2022:**

7:35 p.m. Carol wrote:
What's wrong with Harley? He's carrying those sweets around in three biscuit tins—even when he's onstage as Simple Simon. Now he won't give them to me. This is the closing number. I need to give them out in a couple of minutes.

7:35 p.m. Sarah-Jane wrote:

There are no sweets this year. You'll just have to tell the children Christmas is about more than commerce and they should be happy with good wishes and a few ho-ho-hos.

7:36 p.m. Carol wrote:

There *are* sweets! He's spent the entire play guarding them like a hawk! If he's craving sugar that badly, Harley must be low on nutrients. Have you changed his diet?

7:36 p.m. Sarah-Jane wrote:

He's fine, Mum. DO NOT GIVE OUT THOSE SWEETS. Give out the bags instead.

7:37 p.m. Carol wrote:

Hand out EMPTY bags to children at Christmas? Bags that have "gender-neutral" printed on them?

7:37 p.m. Sarah-Jane wrote:

Yes. Free bags. Much better for their teeth.

---

**Message exchange between Joel and Celia Halliday on December 23, 2022:**

7:43 p.m. Joel wrote:

Oh my days! What have we done? That bloody beanstalk turned out to be a can of worms! Where did it go wrong?

7:45 p.m. Celia wrote:

Can you hear the laughter? The applause? What we've done, my dear, is create a reason for the committee to rethink their ban on *When Did You Last See Your Trousers?* because clearly farce is not dead by a long, long way.

7:46 p.m. Joel wrote:

Good thinking. I like it. We'll resubmit at the earliest opportunity.

7:46 p.m. Celia wrote:

If your name is Halliday, there is no such thing as a plan gone wrong.

---

**Message exchange between Elsie Goodwin and Joyce Walford on December 23, 2022:**

7:46 p.m. Elsie wrote:

Is it over yet, Joyce? You all bowed, we clapped, and the curtain closed, but there seems to be a lot going on still. Where are you?

7:47 p.m. Joyce wrote:

I can't come out yet, Elsie. A terrible thing has happened.

7:49 p.m. Elsie wrote:

Barry just ran past me. I tried to say hello, but he can't have heard. Is he getting a doctor? Is someone ill?

7:54 p.m. Joyce wrote:

Worse. Turns out one of our new members is a police officer.

7:55 p.m. Elsie wrote:

That chap dressed as a bobby was a dead giveaway to me.

7:55 p.m. Joyce wrote:

No, Elsie, that was just Kevin. I can't keep texting you, my Nick needs me.

---

**Message exchange between Denise Malcolm and Marianne Payne on December 23, 2022:**

7:49 p.m. Denise wrote:
I knew there was something familiar about him! He stopped me for a faulty brake light a couple of years ago.

7:49 p.m. Marianne wrote:
Keep quiet, Denise. Don't offer any information, if you know what I mean.

7:50 p.m. Denise wrote:
I don't have any information. Why? Do you?

---

**Message exchange between Sarah-Jane and Kevin MacDonald on December 23, 2022:**

8:12 p.m. Sarah-Jane wrote:
I've sent Harley home with the sweets.

8:14 p.m. Kevin wrote:
Just my luck the place is crawling with cops the one time in my life I've accidentally got something I shouldn't have. Thankfully, they're only interested in the body.

8:15 p.m. Sarah-Jane wrote:
Who'd believe Dustin is a police detective? He was scared of the beanstalk.

8:15 p.m. Kevin wrote:
Thought for a sec he'd arrest me for impersonating a police officer.

8:16 p.m. Sarah-Jane wrote:
You're in the cape and tunic John wore for *Oliver Twist* twenty years ago.

8:16 p.m. Kevin wrote:

Can you sort everything out while I keep my head down? Deal?

8:16 p.m. Sarah-Jane wrote:

That's always the deal, Kevin.

---

To: Sarah-Jane MacDonald
From: Victoria Mayhew
Date: December 23, 2022
Subject: Jack and the Beanstalk

Dear Sarah-Jane,

On behalf of the Mayhew family, may I say how much we all enjoyed The Fairway Players' pantomime and the way you rebooted *Jack and the Beanstalk* for the twenty-first century. We particularly appreciate your:

1. Anti-fracking message, symbolized by a skeleton emerging from a split in the beanstalk, on a sea of unrecyclable packaging.
2. Female-identifying Santa Claus.
3. Free distribution of baked produce to needy children.
4. Gift bags that celebrate gender-neutrality in, literally, as many words.

We, as a family, would like to join The Fairway Players. Please enter our details on your secure database. Merry holidays and Happy Gregorian New Year.

Victoria Mayhew

She/her

**Messages posted to the "Chez MacDonald" WhatsApp group on December 23, 2022:**

**Harley**

I'm home—the sweets are safe

**Kevin**

Harley, Dad's serious now: DO NOT EAT THOSE SWEETS. They're not nice.

**Harley**

they're baggies of cannabis, cocaine, and heroin

**Kevin**

I pay for a good school so you *don't* recognize those sorts of sweets.

**Harley**

only *my* rents would call the feds when they got a stash of cool in their own hutch

**Sarah-Jane**

We didn't call the police. As soon as the curtains closed, the ugly idiot jumped out of character and rang for his "fed" colleagues.

**Sarah-Jane**

Harley, very well done for guarding the SWEETS, making everyone laugh as Simple Simon and facing all this chaos with a clear head. Mum and Dad are very proud of you.

**Harley**

thanks mum it was lit

**Sarah-Jane**

I don't know who that skeleton was or why it was inside the beanstalk, but the police will find out. Good will triumph over evil. Justice will be done.

**Sarah-Jane**

Harley, hide the SWEETS in the loft.

---

To: Celia Halliday
From: Fran Elroy-Jones
Date: December 23, 2022
Subject: The Book of Mormon

Dear Celia,

I've just arrived home and found the envelope you must've popped into my tote bag before the play started. A ticket to see *The Book of Mormon*. Thank you again.

I've texted Greg, who also received a ticket today. I asked if he'd rather take his boyfriend, but apparently neither of them can make that date.

However, you want me to see the show with your son, and I'd like to keep that part of the bargain. Before joining Sainsbury's I worked at a charity that trains ex-prisoners for employment. I'd be there now, if it paid enough for a mortgage. When a former client got too clingy, I knew it was time to make a fresh start.

Your other son, Peter, was in my training group. He's doing very well on his new optometry course and is committed to putting the past behind him. It's just a shame he doesn't have the support of his family. Still, I understand these things are complicated.

Anyway, he'd love to see *The Book of Mormon*, so I've organized to take him instead. Greg will give me his ticket after Christmas.

Thanks again for your generosity, and for all you did to make tonight's pantomime one of the most extraordinary productions I've ever taken part in. Fran

---

To: Sarah-Jane MacDonald
From: Carly & Matthew Dexter
Date: December 23, 2022
Subject: Re: The Fairway Players

Hi Sarah-Jane,
Oh dear! Apologies are in order. We've been decorating one of our houses in Dubai, have only just arrived back in Lockwood and charged up our UK phones. Sorry we missed all your messages. We're still keen to be in the play. Is it too late? Carly & Matt

## County Police Interview Report

Extract from police interview with Joyce Walford, December 24, 2022:

**Sgt. Crowe:** Mrs. Walford, you've come in to speak to us today of your own accord. What would you like to say?

**Mrs. Walford:** That I know who the body in the beanstalk is. Recognized him the minute he flew out with the Fairy Godmother. There wasn't much left to go on, but I knew who it was.

**Sgt. Crowe:** Go on . . .

**Mrs. Walford:** Well . . .

**Charlotte**
No! Why cut the interview off there?

**Femi**
He wants us to work out who the victim was.

**Charlotte**
Ok, so this is a thirty-year-old murder of a man dressed as Father Christmas.

**Femi**
We know Santa Claus traditionally appears at the end of The Fairway Players' pantomime and hands out sweets to the children.

**Charlotte**
And that Joyce's husband, Harry, always used to do it. He died this year, but had played the role for so long Sarah-Jane forgot to enlist someone new.

**Femi**
Which Fairway Players might have been members then? Denise, Joyce, Mick, Marianne, Carol, Joel, and Celia.

**Charlotte**
The Haywards, plus all manner of people from that time who will have left or died.

**Femi**
Wait. Mr. Tanner described this as a mystery. He didn't say murder.

**Charlotte**
The remains were placed inside a stage prop and covered with polystyrene filler. Someone hid the body. Why would they do that, if not to cover up a murder?

**Femi**
Denise points the finger of suspicion at the Hallidays. Is their late-night gathering around the beanstalk a "surprise" for the cast that will also damage the MacDonalds' reputation, or something else: the covering up of a crime committed by their son?

**Charlotte**
But as Joel says, Peter would have been a child when the body was hidden there.

**Femi**
It's not easy to establish cause of death with only skeletal remains, and I'm no expert on how one might dissolve flesh, but perhaps the body is more recent than it might seem?

**Charlotte**
Is the skeleton even real?

**Femi**

Press reports describe it as a "mummified skeleton." Could bones—real or fake—contain contraband, drugs, or diamonds?

**Charlotte**

Gruesome! Let's bring our investigation back to the relationships between The Fairway Players. Denise has a grudge against Celia. I'm not sure we can see her testimony in any other light. Plus, the Hallidays have cut their son Peter out—he's not appeared in their Christmas round-robin for nine years.

**Femi**

The Hallidays go to great lengths to weaken the beanstalk, so that it cracks apart when planned. They wouldn't do that if they knew what was inside it and wanted to keep it secret.

**Charlotte**

But if they knew the body was there and wanted to expose someone else? Someone they *know* to be guilty? The Hallidays are out to get the MacDonalds, any which way they can.

**Femi**

Sarah-Jane wouldn't have brought the beanstalk back to The Fairways if she knew about the body.

**Charlotte**

She says she was a teenager the last time The Fairways staged *Jack and the Beanstalk*.

**Femi**

New member, Dustin Perez, is a secret police officer. Coincidence or undercover?

**Charlotte**

Interesting call. I assumed that was his day job, but you could be right. And if so, who has he been watching?

**Femi**

It surely can't have been anything to do with the body. There must be something else going on in Lockwood.

**Charlotte**

Drugs are being bought and sold.

**Femi**

And a convicted murderer is in the area. Sergeant Crowe confirms that Peter was inside for drug dealing and ABH, but wonders if the Hallidays might have covered up a worse crime for their son.

**Charlotte**

I'm not convinced of that. Anyone who knows what's in the beanstalk can't possibly have anything to do with bringing it back to The Fairways, or opening it up. We should look at who is nervous to see it back.

**Femi**

Joel says to Jock that he thought it had been buried years ago. Buried. Interesting.

**Charlotte**

Asbestos is buried. It's the only legal way to dispose of it.

**Femi**

Yet Joel says he only knew about the asbestos rumors when Denise mentioned them to Celia. Rumors he knows to be unfounded. The murderer-in-town whispers start when the beanstalk shows up.

**Charlotte**

If the community doesn't know what Peter was sent down for, their imaginations would naturally fill in the gaps. Back to Peter again.

**Femi**

In response to Celia's round-robin, Joyce asks whether Peter is still in prison. Joyce also ends up in the police station, claiming to know the identity of the body. Connection?

**Charlotte**

Let's go back to the evidence for our email to Mr. Tanner.

To: Roderick Tanner, KC
From: Femi Hassan & Charlotte Holroyd
Date: November 6, 2023
Subject: Re: A conundrum for you

Dear Mr. Tanner,

The person whose body is concealed in the beanstalk either died while performing the role of Santa Claus or was dressed in the costume postmortem. You've asked us to speculate on who that might be.

Harry Walford was The Fairways' Santa for as long as Sarah-Jane can remember and she clearly states this tradition has happened every year without fail. So we would like to assert that this particular Santa died *after* the pantomime was over that year—the last before Harry took over. Joyce must remember who he took over the role from.

The first mention of asbestos in the documents you sent us was made by Denise Malcolm, who claims she can't recall where or from whom she heard the rumor. The Hallidays have been members just as long, and it was news to them. However, we can't help but notice that Denise mentions Marianne and Joyce as possibly knowing more.

While Marianne and the Payne family are key longtime members of the group, they also seem to move haplessly in low-level criminal circles—Mick asks around to see if anyone he knows can buy sweets in bulk and unwittingly uses an underworld euphemism for drugs. Could they have been equally innocent thirty years ago and inadvertently helped hide a body?

Meanwhile one of the new members, Dustin, is an undercover detective—deployed to infiltrate The Fairway Players and observe the activities of one, or some, of its members. We're not sure who—but we're certain it's not the Paynes or the MacDonalds, as both seem to have been caught up accidentally in the drugs deal. The Hallidays, however, are a different story. Their son has been convicted of drug-related crimes. Beth mentions in her police interview that her parents have various worries, yet Celia sent her annual email on December 1 as usual—reinforcing the impression that nothing is wrong.

When Kevin saw lights on in the church hall, long after the rehearsal had ended, were the Hallidays in there, retrieving something from the beanstalk—something connected to their son Peter—in advance of their trick, designed to ruin the pantomime?

The question remains, however, as to why Joyce would know the identity of the corpse.

Yours sincerely,
Femi Hassan and Charlotte Holroyd

# Messages posted to the WhatsApp group set up by Roderick Tanner, KC, and including Pat Mortimer, Femi Hassan, and Charlotte Holroyd:

**Roderick Tanner, KC**
Your thoughts echo my own at this stage. However, the evidence is best approached with a swipe of Occam's razor.

**Roderick Tanner, KC**
I've posted documents to this What's Up message. Can you see them?

**Charlotte**
Yes! Stop!

**Femi**
You've posted them all three times. The dates are out of sync again. Should we read chronologically or in this order?

**Roderick Tanner, KC**
Read in this order.

# County Police Interview Report

Further extract from police interview with Joyce Walford, December 24, 2022:

**Mrs. Walford:** The body who fell out of the tree is my husband. Was . . .

**Sgt. Crowe:** But Harry Walford died in January of this year. Several people I spoke to said this is the first year they remember without him as Santa.

**Mrs. Walford:** Harry and me were together nearly thirty years. I took his name and so did the boys, but he weren't their dad and we never got married.

**Sgt. Crowe:** Why not?

**Mrs. Walford:** Because legally I were still married to . . . him.

**Sgt. Crowe:** What was his name?

**Mrs. Walford:** Ronnie Bridge.

**Sgt. Crowe:** That rings a bell.

**Mrs. Walford:** I bet it does. He were no stranger to the boys in blue. Spent as much time in your cells as he did at home, as my mother used to say.

**Sgt. Crowe:** Do you know how your husband came to be in the beanstalk?

**Mrs. Walford:** Yeah. It was the last piece of the puzzle. One I've wondered about on and off over the years.

**Sgt. Crowe:** I'm sorry, Mrs. Walford. I can see this is a difficult memory. But can you tell me what happened back then?

**Mrs. Walford:** It were Christmas 1991. We'd done the panto and it'd gone very well, as far as I can remember. Helen was Jack, and Martin played the King. Those were the days, Sergeant—when The Fairway Players were the center of this community. Not now. Anyway, Ronnie had come out dressed as Father Christmas and he'd had a bit to drink. Mums would tell their kids he'd been gargling with Listerine to prepare for his long sleigh journey. I went home early. Nick was a toddler and Barry just a babe-in-arms. My mum was looking after them, back at the apartment. I got in and she went home. Fed the boys, put them to bed, and waited for Ronnie. I waited and waited. You could say I been waiting ever since.

**Sgt. Crowe:** Here, have a tissue, Mrs. Walford. Did you report him missing? For the benefit of the transcript, Mrs. Walford is shaking her head. Take your time, Joyce, there's no hurry.

**Mrs. Walford:** When I woke up in the living room chair the next morning there was a note on the mat. From Ronnie. It explained why he never came home.

**Sgt. Crowe:** Have you still got the note?

**Mrs. Walford:** Tore it up years ago, but I remember his words to this day. "Forgot my key. Will sleep at church hall. See you in the morning. Ron." It was Christmas Eve. I went around to the church hall, but no sign of him. The vicar and the curate searched, Harry and Joel helped, but he was gone. None of us thought to look inside the beanstalk. It was collected later that day by another drama group. Their pantomime started right after Christmas. I know now what must've happened, Officer.

**Sgt. Crowe:** Which was . . . ?

**Mrs. Walford:** It was a cold night. Ron was still wearing his costume. He got inside the beanstalk through the trapdoor, settled down on the warm polystyrene filler and fell asleep. He was a young man, but a heavy drinker and didn't look after himself. For whatever reason, he never woke up. And we were none the wiser.

**Sgt. Crowe:** The next group to use the beanstalk didn't find the body? No one noticed a noxious smell . . . ?

**Mrs. Walford:** I should think when the beanstalk was moved, it shook the body down underneath the filler. Would that have stopped the smell? Maybe that's why they sealed up the trapdoor. Who knows?

**Sgt. Crowe:** Did you report Ronnie missing?

**Mrs. Walford:** Didn't think to. No one came asking for him, except the usual.

**Sgt. Crowe:** The usual?

**Mrs. Walford:** People he owed money to. Old business associates. Concerned family members. No one who thought he'd gone anywhere other than off with another woman. My mum told everyone he'd scarpered, leaving debts galore and me on my own with two little 'uns. Too cowardly to tell me to my face. She said it so many times I ended up believing it. When I saw him come out the beanstalk yesterday . . . I realized the silly old boot was wrong. He'd gone to sleep in the church hall, like he said. Gone to sleep and died in The Fairways' Santa suit that he'd just worn to make the local children happy . . . Sorry, Sergeant. I can't help it.

**Sgt. Crowe:** Here, have another tissue. What happened next? As the days went by and no Ronnie?

**Mrs. Walford:** Well, you dry your eyes and pick yourself up. I had my boys to think of, so I got on with it—and a good job I did, because before long, Harry and I were together. I don't like to speak ill of the dead, especially not when their passing was accidental and tragic, but Harry was ten times the man Ronnie ever was—and ten times the father to Nick and Barry.

**Sgt. Crowe:** Do the boys know?

**Mrs. Walford:** Do they know what?

**Sgt. Crowe:** The story you've just told me.

**Mrs. Walford:** Of course I told them Harry weren't their dad.

**Sgt. Crowe:** What do they know about their real dad?

**Mrs. Walford:** The truth is, we don't talk about it. Not the bad memories. You focus on the good things—that's the way to live.

**Sgt. Crowe:** You may be right there, Joyce.

**Mrs. Walford:** When us Walfords find an obstacle, we pick it up, give it a wink, then a kick out the park.

**Sgt. Crowe:** Do you now.

**Mrs. Walford:** Well, Officer, I'd better be getting home. Barry's new girlfriend is coming for dinner tomorrow—it's their first Christmas together—and the turkey needs putting on a low light—

**Sgt. Crowe:** Mrs. Walford, we aren't quite finished. When Nick and Barry saw the body emerge from the beanstalk, when did they realize it was their biological father?

**Mrs. Walford:** Like I said. A lot of things are unspoken in families, aren't they?

**Sgt. Crowe:** I see. They don't know.

**Message exchange between DS Dustin Perez and Sarah-Jane MacDonald on December 24, 2022:**

3:46 p.m. Dustin wrote:
Do you know a Ronald Bridge?

3:46 p.m. Sarah-Jane wrote:
Why? What has he said?

3:47 p.m. Dustin wrote:
He's a former Fairway Player from many decades ago.

3:49 p.m. Sarah-Jane wrote:
Sorry! Yes, my mother is here helping prepare for tomorrow, and she remembers Ronnie Bridge. Apparently he was Joyce's first husband, who ran off with another woman.

3:50 p.m. Dustin wrote:
In 1991, on the night of The Fairways' panto, we believe he was locked out, crawled into the beanstalk to sleep and, sadly, died. We've yet to receive the official autopsy, but it seems he was drunk on the spirit of Christmas and sank beneath the polystyrene filler either before or after he breathed his last. Concerns over asbestos meant that soon afterward the trapdoor was screwed shut and sealed with filler, creating an airless cavity inside. Polystyrene absorbs moisture slowly, and over the years the remains were effectively mummified.

3:55 p.m. Sarah-Jane wrote:
I can't tell you how relieved I am, Officer Perez.

3:55 p.m. Sarah-Jane wrote:
I mean, that is absolutely tragic. How is Joyce taking it?

3:56 p.m. Dustin wrote:
Mrs. Walford is very stoical. However, Nick and Barry still don't realize the skeletal remains that burst out of a stage beanstalk in a Santa suit, and swept them off their feet as they were dressed as a pantomime cow, was actually their biological father. I'd appreciate it if you kept those details to yourself for now.

3:59 p.m. Sarah-Jane wrote:
Well, it's good news the family has closure and he can rest in peace. RIP. Dustin, would you like to audition for the next play? If so, keep the second week in January free.

---

**Message exchange between Carol Dearing and Denise Malcolm on December 24, 2022:**

4:04 p.m. Carol wrote:
You'll never guess who that skeleton was, Denise. Nasty old Ronnie Bridge. I'm at Sarah-Jane's. She's had a tip-off from the police.

4:06 p.m. Denise wrote:
They say bad pennies always show up eventually. Funny he should come back just as Harry dies. As if he was afraid before, and now he's back to claim his woman.

4:08 p.m. Carol wrote:
Imagine being afraid of dopey old Harry and, for that matter, imagine Joyce being a prize worth fighting for! And with that, I'll say a Happy Christmas to you and yours, Denise.

4:10 p.m. Denise wrote:

You are awful, Carol. I'm choking on my mince pie here! Happy
Christmas to you, too!

---

To: Sarah-Jane MacDonald
From: Rev. Joshua Harries
Date: December 24, 2022
Subject: Wall panel

Dear Mrs. MacDonald,

The police have just cleared away their cordon and finally allowed
me back into the church hall. Having searched high and low, I
eventually discovered the wall panel underneath an old shopping
cart. It is snapped in two, covered in goodness-knows-what and
shoved at the back of the cloakroom cupboard. Tragically, it is beyond repair.

I hope and pray the pantomime has raised enough money for
a new one. Unfortunately, as a result of this, I must rethink the
tenure of The Fairway Players in our church hall.

May I wish you a merry Christmas and peaceful New Year.
Yours, Rev. Harries

P.S. My thoughts are with the group member who passed away in
the beanstalk.

# County Police Debrief Report

Extract from the transcription of Detective Sergeant Dustin Perez's debriefing with Inspector Cooper, January 11, 2023:

**Insp. Cooper:** Can you summarize the job, DS? Cheers.

**DS Perez:** I was deployed into the Lockwood community to observe a couple suspected of moving contraband, in the form of drugs, through the supply chain. I occupied an apartment in the new public housing and made myself known to locals as a shy, gentle, slightly nervous bachelor who enjoyed amateur drama.

**Insp. Cooper:** Why amateur drama?

**DS Perez:** I've taken part in amateur drama my whole life, Sergeant. I know the scene. I know the people. How they think. How these organizations work. The Fairway Players is an active community group. It was a good place from which to observe comings and goings. Intel had reached us the suspected couple were members. I just didn't know which couple.

**Insp. Cooper:** I understand you auditioned for—and won—a part in the panto.

**DS Perez:** I was initially cast as a giant fairy, but later promoted to the ugly idiot.

**Insp. Cooper:** Apologies for laughing, DS. Not sure if congratulations are in order or not.

**DS Perez:** The script was written in the 1970s.

**Insp. Cooper:** And did any of the couples arouse your suspicions?

**DS Perez:** There were three contenders: the Paynes, the MacDonalds, and the Hallidays. The last two direct and produce alternate productions and have no prior convictions themselves, although the Hallidays' eldest son, Peter, was released from prison last year after a series of short sentences for petty offenses.

**Insp. Cooper:** I understand they're estranged . . .

**DS Perez:** The Hallidays are very protective of their status in the community. Apparently Peter is estranged even from the family's Christmas round-robin, let alone the house. Meanwhile the Paynes are foot soldiers of the drama group, helping out with set building and costumes, etc.—no previous offenses themselves. However, Mick Payne's brother has a rap sheet for drug offenses.

**Insp. Cooper:** Interesting . . .

**DS Perez:** So, as I worked my way into the group, I became immersed in my part.

**Insp. Cooper:** Careful, DS. It's easier than you think to become the role you play.

**DS Perez:** The giant fairy or the ugly idiot?

**Insp. Cooper:** I mean the role of shy, gentle, nervous bachelor who enjoys amateur drama. Stockholm Syndrome. Going native. Whatever they like to call it now.

**DS Perez:** Ah, no. Not at all. I maintained a position of distant objectivity the whole time.

**Insp. Cooper:** Good . . .

**DS Perez:** Except when rumors reached me that the beanstalk could contain asbestos. Health and safety are paramount when undercover, Sergeant. From then on, I maintained a position of distant objectivity from the beanstalk.

**Insp. Cooper:** Understandable.

**DS Perez:** The beanstalk turned out to contain something worse than asbestos, if not as dangerous.

**Insp. Cooper:** The body of Ronald Bridge. A very sad affair.

**DS Perez:** His family now has closure and he can be laid to rest. May flights of angels sing him to his rest, and all that.

**Insp. Cooper:** Bridge had a string of convictions for violent offenses, most of which were against his wife, Joyce.

**DS Perez:** May he rot in Hell.

**Insp. Cooper:** His disappearance thirty years ago was a perfect storm. Everyone thought he'd gone somewhere else of his own accord, and no one expected to hear from him again. You've got to feel sorry for the boys, though. They didn't know the body was their father.

**DS Perez:** I understand Joyce came in and volunteered the intel?

**Insp. Cooper:** She did. A solid type. Salt of the earth. Straight-talking usually . . . only not on this matter. She simply couldn't tell those boys—grown men now—that the body was their flesh and blood.

**DS Perez:** She did eventually, Sergeant. I was there when she told them.

**Insp. Cooper:** When was this?

**DS Perez:** Last night. At the first audition for the next play. I was at the tea counter with Joyce and asked her how the boys took the news.

**Insp. Cooper:** Careful, DS, she'll wonder how you know.

**DS Perez:** Everyone knows. It was the talk of the audition. When she said she still hadn't told them, I couldn't believe they hadn't heard through the grapevine.

**Insp. Cooper:** Gossip's funny like that.

**DS Perez:** Joyce said she didn't want to ruin their Christmas, then their New Year. She hadn't gotten around to it. "Joyce," I said, "you have to tell them. They need to know." She looks me in the eye, all teary and says, "Yes, Dustin—you're a copper, will you help?"

**Insp. Cooper:** And you said yes.

**DS Perez:** Of course. She called Nick and Barry into the props cupboard. I held her hand. She said she had something to tell them.

**Insp. Cooper:** How did they take it?

**DS Perez:** Nick, the eldest, he was silent for a moment or two, while it sank in. Then he hugged his mother and said his dad would've been stoked to know he was still playing Santa so many years later. The younger son, Barry, he was more emotional. Said he was planning to propose to his girlfriend, and now his real dad would never get to meet her.

**Insp. Cooper:** That's sad . . .

**DS Perez:** That's when the tears came.

**Insp. Cooper:** What happened then?

**DS Perez:** I dried my eyes, we held our heads up, went back out into the church hall and carried on with the rehearsal.

**Insp. Cooper:** And the couple rumored to be running a drugs business from the heart of The Fairway Players?

**DS Perez:** Couldn't see any evidence of it. Must be dodgy intel.

I did hear something interesting, that a convicted murderer is "back in Lockwood." In light of that, I've decided to stay on as a member of The Fairway Players.

**Insp. Cooper:** Are you sure, DS?

**DS Perez:** I can't leave now. I've been cast as Captain Webber in *When Did You Last See Your Trousers?*

**Charlotte**

So *Jack and the Beanstalk* turned from a pantomime into a farce and then into a Christmas tragedy. How sad.

**Femi**

The "tragedy" happened thirty years ago.

**Charlotte**

For Joyce, Nick, and Barry, it's happening now. Yet Joyce says, "You focus on the good things—that's the way to live." That's out of character. Look back at her reply to Celia's round-robin, right at the start: she's The Fairway Players' most fatalistic member.

**Femi**

People say, and do, uncharacteristic things when they're shocked or grieving. Barry says to Myra, "Love you, babe. Remember that, yeah?" Which is unusually emotional for him.

**Charlotte**

Notice what Joyce says next in her interview: "When us Walfords find an obstacle, we pick it up, give it a wink, then a kick out the park." That's a close paraphrase of Celia's round-robin.

**Femi**
Let's not make assumptions before we look back over what the Walfords said, and did, during rehearsals.

**Charlotte**
The Walford boys help paint the beanstalk and do a good job.

**Femi**
Joyce volunteers them. She says their dad was a painter and decorator.

**Charlotte**
She wants the beanstalk to stay exactly where it is onstage.

**Femi**
During the ill-fated performance she messages her friend Elsie that she needs to "make sure" of something. It can't be where the boys are, like she says, because they're onstage.

**Charlotte**
It's possible she suspects the beanstalk contains her husband's body.

**Femi**
Suspects or knows?

**Charlotte**

We see Joyce snap at Sarah-Jane when she says she takes back everything she's said about the boys. SJ sometimes speaks before she thinks, but her attitude to Nick and Barry seems to reflect their poor reputation within the community.

**Femi**

Boys. We call them boys, like everyone here, but they're both over thirty.

**Charlotte**

Their reputation isn't unearned. We see them hide a can of beer to drink secretly during the show.

**Femi**

Before that, they're drunk at rehearsals.

**Charlotte**

Anyone would be concerned about this behavior in their adult sons, but Joyce must remember the effect alcohol had on their father, and worry they may be taking the same path. Is it any wonder she doesn't tell them the true identity of the body in the beanstalk?

**Femi**

And who is the convicted murderer? We hear Peter Halliday was released, but Sergeant Crowe states that was for drugs offenses and actual bodily harm.

**Charlotte**
I can understand why he's missing from the Hallidays' round-robin every year. Celia and Joel are keen to replace the Haywards as the power family of Lockwood.

**Femi**
A convicted murderer is back in town, and Sarah-Jane isn't at all concerned. Is this because she knows who it is?

**Charlotte**
Or are the MacDonalds really the "drugs couple" that DS Perez was shadowing? He's looking for people who move drugs through the supply chain. Business people, not street-level dealers.

**Femi**
True. And such people tend to be outwardly respectable members of the community.

**Charlotte**
If it's the MacDonalds, then their dismay at being in possession of class A drugs would have to be faked. That way, if their communications are ever seized, they can claim innocence. Let's read on?

To: Sarah-Jane MacDonald
From: Isabel Beck
Date: January 12, 2023
Subject: Hiya!

Hey, SJ! OMG! When I saw the headline "Body in the Beanstalk" I had no idea the story would be about the drama group I used to be a member of! What a coincidence!

That must have been quite a surprise for everyone onstage. Did you manage to work it into the play? In *Blithe Spirit*, when I had to put a whole tea set on a tray while saying my lines, I forgot the sugar bowl, so nipped back onstage later to collect it. I made up a couple of lines to account for the sudden reappearance of Edith the Maid. No one in the audience noticed.

I often think back to my time as a Fairway Player. Happy memories! Of course after all the hoo-hah that went on, I do have one regret—that I wasn't a member long enough to be in a panto. How cool would that have been! I like to think that if a body came out of a beanstalk while I was onstage, I'd have been quite calm. You may remember I used to work in a geriatric ward—death was my bread and butter back then, but not anymore!

Guess what I'm up to now, SJ? Well, I was stuck for a while, wondering what I could do that was like nursing, but not nursing, if you know what I mean. Then, whoosh! My social worker put me in touch with the Prison Optician Trust and, to cut a long story short, I'm almost a fully qualified optician!

It was all thanks to Fran Elroy-Jones, who started off as my case worker at the charity and is now my best friend. Even though she's not there anymore, we're still close and stay in regular touch.

Of course I don't talk about my time in Lockwood, as it's all water under the bridge, so she didn't realize I had history there. Imagine my surprise when I finally discovered where she'd gone! And not only that, but she'd joined The Fairway Players! It's uncanny, like we're secret sisters or something. But that's not the only coincidence! While she was mentoring me, someone else joined our group and I thought: That's a familiar name. It was Peter Halliday! I didn't even realize Celia and Joel had another son—but he was in prison for possession, intent to supply, and actual bodily harm. Not that I can tell anyone, as details like that are strictly confidential. I stay in touch with him, as he still meets up with Fran. We're like the Three Musketeers!

A couple of weeks ago I put on a big coat and went to Lockwood, just for an afternoon, to see Fran in her new job and apartment. I know I shouldn't go back, because that's what the social workers told me when I was released, but I thought: Well, that's all in the past now and I have the perfect excuse, if anyone asks. Fran lives on Hayward Heights, parks her car in a reserved bay, and works at Sainsbury's. In the offices, not the aisles. It was so lovely to see her again.

Unfortunately, while I was crouched behind a shelving unit, I bumped into Denise Malcolm, who seemed confused that I was out and about. Not everyone keeps up with the latest news! Speaking of which, Lockwood has changed so much in the last couple of years. The new public housing estates are enormous and there are so many more people in town. I hope that means bigger audiences for Fairways and lots of new members!

How is everyone? Harley must be fourteen or fifteen now! OMG, almost grown-up! And you, SJ? All the newspaper articles about the pantomime say you're a mother of two. Gasp! Does that mean you've had a baby? Congratulations (if so)!

Well, I'd better go. I've got to study for exams at the end of this month, boo! It's my dream now to have my own optics practice in Lockwood. Perhaps Peter and I can go into business together. There's a thought! Lots of love, Issy

---

**Message exchange between Sarah-Jane and Kevin MacDonald on January 12, 2023:**

4:33 p.m. Sarah-Jane wrote:
I was right about the "convicted murderer back in town" rumors. Isabel Beck.

4:41 p.m. Kevin wrote:
No way, José! Don't suppose she learned how to distribute a shedload of class A drugs while inside, did she?

4:43 p.m. Sarah-Jane wrote:
Now the dust has settled on the whole pantomime affair, that's my next project. Leave it with me.

---

**Message exchange between Sarah-Jane MacDonald and Jade's phone on January 12, 2023:**

4:56 p.m. Sarah-Jane MacDonald wrote:
Hi, Jade. Happy New Year and all that. Just a quick question. Would you happen to know anyone who could take some green, white, and brown SWEETS off my hands? If you get my hidden meaning. Despite working in high-level marketing for years, I have absolutely no contacts in that line of business myself. I wonder if, by any chance, you do?

4:59 p.m. Jade's phone wrote:

You think, because I live on the new public housing estate, I must run around with drug-dealing lowlife? I have to watch every penny, but I'd never get involved in anything like that. Being a single mum is hard enough, without people branding you a criminal, too.

5:11 p.m. Sarah-Jane MacDonald wrote:

I'm so sorry. I certainly didn't mean that how it sounded. Of course I understand life can be hard, and I respect anyone who battles through against the odds. You have my sincere apologies.

5:14 p.m. Jade's phone wrote:

Ha-ha! Had you there, Sarah. Only kidding. Mate of a mate will take the green and white off your hands. He won't touch brown, though. Won't even have it in the house. You're caught with that, he says, you're sent down for a LONG time. I can ask around, though.

5:15 p.m. Sarah-Jane MacDonald wrote:

That is such a relief, Jade, thank you.

5:17 p.m. Jade's phone wrote:

No worries. Nice of you to get us into the panto. The kids are still talking about Halloween Santa on his flying carpet.

5:22 p.m. Sarah-Jane MacDonald wrote:

Jade, please tell your friend I don't want any money for the drugs. Can he make a donation to charity or something?

5:22 p.m. Sarah-Jane MacDonald wrote:

SWEETS! I mean "sweets." Class A sweets.

5:25 p.m. Jade's phone wrote:

Charity? I can tell you don't have many friends in that business, Sarah. I'll make sure some cash gets to a few needy families on the estate. Things are hard now, what with prices going up and everything. Will ask him if he knows someone who'll take the brown off your hands.

5:29 p.m. Sarah-Jane MacDonald wrote:

Thank you, thank you, thank you, Jade. I'll drop the green and white sweets off now.

---

**Message exchange between Carly Dexter and Sarah-Jane MacDonald on January 13, 2023:**

11:23 a.m. Carly Dexter wrote:

Hello, Sarah-Jane. My apologies for the mix-up over the play. I've read back over your emails and can see my husband and I let you and The Fairway Players down badly over the pantomime roles. We were called overseas unexpectedly and should have told you. We feel terrible, but it's been brought to our attention how we might make amends. Word reached us that you have an exotic consignment you would like to move. This is our business, and we are happy to help.

11:29 a.m. Sarah-Jane MacDonald wrote:

Really? That's wonderful news, Carly. Please don't worry about letting us down. Yes, you've heard correctly. It's a long story, but I am in reluctant possession of some BROWN SWEETS. I'll bring them around to yours asap.

11:29 a.m. Sarah-Jane MacDonald wrote:

On second thoughts, I'll send my husband, Kevin. We don't want any money, just to be rid of the goods.

11:33 a.m. Carly Dexter wrote:

In that case, we'll make a significant donation to the church hall roof fund—in lieu of the inconvenience our sudden absence caused.

---

**Messages posted to the "Chez MacDonald" WhatsApp group on January 13, 2023:**

**Kevin**

I'm home. It's done. The handover went smoothly. The eagle has landed.

**Sarah-Jane**

The pantomime is over. Finally.

**Kevin**

Still don't know what went wrong.

**Sarah-Jane**

No, Kevin. It went right. Celia and Joel planned to disrupt the show, but the MacDonalds faced every challenge that came their way, picked it up, gave it a wink, and firmly knocked it out of the park.

**Harley**

what you on about mum

**Sarah-Jane**

Nothing. Now, let's all pull together to make *When Did You Last See Your Trousers?* our best play yet!

---

To: Sarah-Jane MacDonald
From: Rev. Joshua Harries
Date: January 15, 2023
Subject: Next play

Dear Mrs. MacDonald,
You will be delighted to know that, thanks to the generous donation made on behalf of your group, we have been able to repair the roof and replace the wall panel. We also have some money left over for further maintenance to the church hall.

May I say how much I am looking forward to The Fairway Players' next production. Yours, Rev. Harries

Clipping from the *Lockwood Gazette*, January 23, 2023:

## BODY IN THE BEANSTALK
## MYSTERY SOLVED

The so-called body-in-the-beanstalk mystery is finally solved, according to a statement by local police. The male, found in a Santa suit and in an advanced state of decomposition, is now known to have been sealed inside a pantomime beanstalk after a tragic chain of events thirty years ago. His unconventional resting place was only discovered on December 23 last year, during a performance of *Jack and the Beanstalk* by The Fairway Players, in Lockwood.

After appearing as Father Christmas in the drama group's pantomime of 1991, local decorator Ronald Bridge, then thirty-nine and a father of two, posted a note through the mail slot to say he had forgotten his keys and would spend the night in the church hall. This note was all Joyce Bridge had left of her husband until last month, when the aging beanstalk broke apart and his petrified skeleton emerged onto the stage.

Police now say he must have crawled into the beanstalk to keep warm, but passed away sud-

denly and unexpectedly overnight. The structure was subsequently sealed up, over fears it
contained asbestos, and has since been used nu-
merous times by local drama groups who often
stage the traditional pantomime at Christmas
and New Year.

"Everyone assumed he'd run off with another woman," Mrs. Bridge said, "which just
goes to show it was his own fault."

Cochair of The Fairway Players, mother
of two Sarah-Jane MacDonald, is quoted
as saying, "The pantomime this year had a
rather surprising and macabre plot twist, but
in the end we improvised and, thanks to the
quick-thinking ingenuity of cast and crew, we
made it work. I don't remember Ron myself,
but he was a Fairway Player and, like anyone involved in the theater, he will have relished the
idea that he could still raise a laugh and a cheer
so many years after his death. I'm also relieved
for the family that they can now say a proper
goodbye to their long-lost husband and father.
If anyone reading this would like to become a
member of The Fairway Players, I would urge
them to visit our website and sign up. We are a
friendly, welcoming group, open to all."

**Femi**
The "convicted murderer" is Isabel Beck. That's why SJ isn't concerned.

**Charlotte**
Some mud always sticks, even when a conviction is overturned.

**Femi**
With the accidental drugs haul dispersed, it's a nice, neat ending to a macabre Christmas story. But why is Mr. Tanner showing us all this? What is it about this open-and-shut case he wants us to spot?

**Charlotte**
There's only one way to find out.

# Messages posted to the WhatsApp group set up by Roderick Tanner, KC, and including Pat Mortimer, Femi Hassan, and Charlotte Holroyd:

**Femi**
We've read everything you sent, Mr. Tanner.

**Pat M**
What's this about a body in a beanstalk?

**Roderick Tanner, KC**
What do you know about it?

**Pat M**
Nothing. You sent me these pages of talk about a body. I thought it was an internet joke and read them all. There's no punch line, just a sad ending. Are you playing golf next week or what?

**Roderick Tanner, KC**
Patrick Mortimer, those are confidential documents meant for my former students and no one else.

**Pat M**
Well, don't send them to me then!

**Pat Mortimer has left the group.**

**Roderick Tanner, KC**

I apologize. I had no idea random people could jump into a conversation like that.

**Charlotte**

Adding someone accidentally to a WhatsApp group is easily done.

**Roderick Tanner, KC**

Thankfully this isn't an active legal case, so even if my long-term golf partner had infiltrated the group, it wouldn't have compromised anything. What do you make of it?

**Femi**

Thank you for these further documents, Mr. Tanner. They throw light on some earlier events. In particular, the identity of the corpse, but if this isn't an active case, why do you have these documents?

**Roderick Tanner, KC**

A worried party contacted their lawyer before the coroner's verdict and the process of e-discovery was set in motion, but in the end they were not required and the documents abandoned. Other than that, let's just say I have an entire career's worth of police and legal contacts. However, you must be aware that we three are the only people who can see ALL these documents. Everyone else has access to merely a selection.

**Charlotte**

What do you want us to do with them? Confirm your suspicions, like before?

**Roderick Tanner, KC**

Not quite. I need you to reassure me that I am right in keeping these documents well away from anyone who might be able to act upon their contents. There are some instances where justice is served by not troubling the legal system.

**Femi**

So you think Ronnie Bridge's death wasn't a tragic accident—but that killing him was the right thing to do?

**Roderick Tanner, KC**

I have a few final documents for you to read. I'll send them by email, not this confounded What's Up thing.

**Messages posted to the "Mum and us" WhatsApp group on December 2, 2022:**

**Joyce**

What's it look like?

**Nick**

Heavy as fuck. The four of us could only just carry it.

**Joyce**

Can you see the trapdoor?

**Nick**

No. It's been sealed up and plastered over. You'd have to know it was there, to notice it.

**Joyce**

Good.

**And on December 12, 2022:**

**Joyce**

I've said you'll paint it. Make sure the trapdoor is invisible. We don't want that lot suddenly deciding to open it.

**Barry**

But I'm taking Myra to the dog races for a special night.

**Joyce**

You can go out with Myra anytime. Make sure it's done properly. You know what I mean.

**Message exchange between Denise Malcolm and Joyce Walford on December 12, 2022:**

12:35 p.m. Denise wrote:
Tell your Nick and Barry to stay well away from the beanstalk, Joyce. It's full of asbestos. Sarah-Jane doesn't want anyone to know.

12:36 p.m. Joyce wrote:
How do you know what it's full of?

12:39 p.m. Denise wrote:
Your Harry said. Years ago, when it was here last. Marianne and I helped him take it to the Mendham Players and he whispered it to them. He told them he'd sealed up the trapdoor, so no one could breathe it in. What a hero! Get your lads to wear masks if they go anywhere near it.

12:44 p.m. Joyce wrote:
I will, Denise—you can't be too careful.

---

**Messages posted to the "Mum and us" WhatsApp group on December 18, 2022:**

**Joyce**
Get away from the beanstalk. Don't draw attention to it.

**Barry**
Just doing a little dance.

**Joyce**
In that cow suit?

**Barry**

Yeah! Ha-ha-ha!

**Joyce**

You two been drinking?

**And on December 23, 2022:**

**Joyce**

For God's sake, look surprised, Nick.

**Nick**

I've got my cow head on.

**Later:**

**Nick**

Play it straight, Mum, and this'll be the end of it. No more worrying about where that beanstalk is, or when he'll be found. This is the best thing that could've happened.

**Barry**

Yeah, won't be hanging over us anymore.

**Then on January 10, 2023:**

**Joyce**

Listen, the cop's sniffing about. I've said I'll tell you now.

**Barry**

Just say Harry musta done it. He's dead now—what's the harm in that?

**Joyce**

I'm not having my Harry's name sullied. All he did was help afterward.

**Barry**

You're in the clear, Mum. No one thinks it's you.

**Nick**

Can't be too careful, Baz. These things look different to outsiders.

**Joyce**

Too right they do. They didn't know Ronnie. He went for me one time too many. All I did was kick him into that beanstalk and jam the trapdoor shut, determined a night in there would make him think about his drinking. I told Joel that Ron had already left, so we locked up and went home.

**Nick**

I'll speak to Mr. Junker anyway. He's a diamond lawyer who's got me out of a few scrapes. He can start getting our ducks in a row. Just in case, eh?

**Barry**

We know you didn't mean to, Mum.

**Joyce**

That's right; it weren't my fault no one could hear his shouts for help. Next morning I told Joel I'd left my purse backstage and got the key to the church hall. Opened the trapdoor and there was Ronnie, the old fucker, still in his Santa suit, dead as a doornail.

**Nick**

What a bastard!

**Joyce**

Must've suffocated. I ran straight to Harry. He sent me off shopping
to town, so I'd have an alibi, while he screwed the trapdoor shut, got
Denise and Marianne to help him take the beanstalk to Mendham's.
Turns out he also started the rumor it's full of asbestos, to explain why
it was sealed.

**Barry**

It could happen to anyone, that.

**Joyce**

I've told the cops Ronnie was pissed and must've choked on the filler,
so if their scientists can tell he was suffocated while tipsy, it'll all add
up for them. They needn't know any inconvenient detail.

**Nick**

Anyone who remembers him would say he deserved what he got.
Good riddance.

**Joyce**

Boys, there's one final thing we gotta do, and you've been members of
The Fairways long enough to pull it off. All that's left is to convince this
soppy cop.

**Barry**

You sure, Mum? He might be one of those clever cops, like Officer
Dibble.

**Joyce**

I've done my bit down at the station, now it's your turn. Just act the grieving sons. You can do it.

**Barry**

Ok, I'm in.

**Nick**

Let's nail this.

**Later:**

**Joyce**

He's crying his eyes out. I'll tell you what, never mind the bloody Hallidays—us Walfords can face every challenge and that's for sure! Well done, boys!

# WhatsApp group set up by Roderick Tanner, KC, and including Femi Hassan and Charlotte Holroyd:

**Femi**

So Joyce killed her abusive husband. There was no note to say he was sleeping in the church hall. Harry hid the body in the beanstalk. This is a case of unlawful death, after all.

**Charlotte**

It seems strange Harry should enlist Denise and Marianne to help him move a large, heavy beanstalk. Surely there were bigger, stronger men around to help.

**Femi**

It's possible at least one of them knew then what was in it, even if Joyce didn't realize it. And if they knew in 1991, they still know now.

**Charlotte**

Early in the rehearsal schedule, on December 4, Dustin overhears Joyce and Marianne talking about "what happened" and thinks they mean the change in leadership—the hot potato of current group politics. Sarah-Jane assumes they were discussing the appeal case we worked on. But maybe their topic of conversation was something that "happened" much earlier . . .

**Femi**

Well spotted. They could easily have been getting their story straight, should the contents of the beanstalk be revealed.

**Charlotte**

How did you get these documents, Mr. Tanner? They constitute a confession.

**Roderick Tanner, KC**

They came to light. My colleague disregarded them. Was he right?

**Charlotte**

You want us to disregard them, too. Forget we ever read this—like you have.

**Femi**

You're retired, but we're just starting our careers. We can't let this slide.

**Roderick Tanner, KC**

If the "victim" is killed in self-defense, it carries a "not guilty" verdict.

**Femi**

Maybe, but the evidence needs to go through the court for the case to be found as such. It's by no means certain Joyce didn't know exactly what she was doing when she kicked Ronnie into the beanstalk and locked the trapdoor.

**Charlotte**

She says no one heard his shouts for help, which indicates that she heard them, but deliberately left him there.

**Femi**

Suppressing this evidence is abuse of process. We can't ignore these documents, Mr. Tanner. If you don't go to the police, then Charlotte and I will.

**Roderick Tanner, KC**

That's enough! I have a final piece of information for you: a nice surprise after all your hard work. The autopsy findings. In short, Ronald Bridge died from alcohol-induced blood poisoning. The pathologist declared "death by natural causes." Natural causes of Ronnie's own making, I might add. Whatever Joyce thinks she did all those years ago, it didn't kill him. Harry was guilty of preventing a burial, but he's dead himself now.

**Charlotte**

So it's *not* an unlawful death?

**Roderick Tanner, KC**
All's well that ends well.

**Femi**
You played a trick on us.

**Roderick Tanner, KC**
More a test. Not of your skills of deduction, which I know to be exemplary, but of your attitude to professional conduct. A test, I am delighted to say, you've both passed.

**Charlotte**
Shouldn't the Walfords be told that their husband and father died of natural causes?

**Roderick Tanner, KC**
I rather like how mother and sons bond over their shared secret. As do The Fairway Players. These invisible ties keep us together, do they not?

**Charlotte**
If Joyce and Harry kept this secret for years, then potentially other Fairway Players did, too.

**Femi**
It isn't entirely clear who knows about the body and who doesn't.

**Roderick Tanner, KC**
I suspect the clues to that are buried deep in this
bundle of correspondence, never to be revealed.

**Charlotte**
Wake up! Femi! Are you awake?

**Femi**
Haven't been to bed. So much work . . .

**Charlotte**
The body in the beanstalk was a mummified
SKELETON. You can't get blood-alcohol levels
from bones and skin. I've got the coroner's report
here. "Due to the advanced state of the remains,
exact cause of death could not be ascertained.
Open verdict."

**Femi**
So Bridge may have died of alcohol poisoning, the
way Mr. Tanner said, or may have died of suffocation
as a result of Joyce's action, as she believes. We'll
never know.

**Charlotte**
Mr. Tanner was always a maverick, right? But this
time he's *lied* to stop us referring the case—and
him.

**Femi**
He's retired. No longer constrained by professional standards.

**Charlotte**
Still calls himself KC. How can we trust him now?

**Femi**
Think about where he is. He's bored and restless, and for the first time he can see his entire career. All the places he went wrong and the things he could have done better.

**Charlotte**
You think he's compensating for something we know nothing about? A case where the outcome was "just" but not "right"?

**Femi**
We have a choice: refer the case or forget we ever read those final messages.

**Charlotte**
We must both agree.

**Femi**
And take equal responsibility for the decision.

**Charlotte**

I don't want to trouble a system overloaded with a crippling backlog for the sake of a long-dead wife beater. One whose own actions contributed at least as much to his death as anyone else's actions. But I never want to forget that I didn't say anything, or why.

**Femi**

When and if the time is ever right, we can discuss it again and, if we both agree, open the can of worms. We have that option. Agreed?

**Charlotte**

Agreed.

To: [Address List]
From: Sarah-Jane MacDonald
Date: December 24, 2022
Subject: Round-robin

Dear all,

Before I begin, I must thank my mother, without whose regular reminders every year I would probably never write another Christmas round-robin again. As far as I can see, it is an exercise in wishful thinking at best, and at worst an attempt to delude oneself and others. I am not averse to tradition, it's just that some traditions are more worthy of continuation than others. The only good thing about the round-robin is that it gives one a platform to speak one's mind unchallenged. Here goes.

I have never been prouder of my family than when the worst happens and they muddle through. And when I say "my family" I don't mean just Harley, Sammy, and Kevin. I mean The Fairway Players. Because family means those around us who share our world, not only those in our home or on our Christmas list. We do not always see eye-to-eye. In fact, at times we simply cannot stand the sight of each other—but when something awful happens to one of us, it happens to all of us, and we all help to remove the hurdle or leap over it.

Theatrical people say, "The show must go on." Well, that is true of life, is it not?

This year we faced some challenges that included the postponement of *An Evening with Gary Lineker* when the church hall roof collapsed under the weight of a bat patty. The new dates meant Nick Walford was on a stag weekend and unable to play Gary Lineker, OBE. The only person able to stand in was Nick's sixty-seven-year-old mother, Joyce. Despite being particularly scathing about the former footballer and TV pundit, she got up onstage and inhabited the character—and his football uniform— to the best of her abilities.

Later in the year, when our pantomime *Jack and the Beanstalk* turned out to be a rather gruesome collision of past and present, it emerged that many years ago The Fairway Players were a similarly close-knit team who came together to support each other when the need arose. It's clear that our sense of duty and comradeship never dies and that family—whatever it may mean to you—is a bond that stretches beyond our blood ties to those we share our precious time on earth with.

That, for me, is the true meaning of Christmas.

With festive greetings and warmest wishes for the New Year,

Sarah-Jane, Kevin, Harley, and Samantha

# Acknowledgments

Before late summer 2022 I had no inclination to revisit the world of *The Appeal*. When my exceptionally talented UK editor, Miranda Jewess, mentioned that a Christmas story might be an interesting adventure, I still didn't realize it would be with The Fairway Players. However, the moment I started to write, the story took me straight back to Lockwood.

It felt like visiting old friends, peeking between curtains and under rugs, discovering the twists and turns that have shaped these characters' worlds in the three years since *The Appeal* was published. I hope you enjoy reading about their exploits as much as I enjoyed writing about them.

This project was codenamed *Beanstalk* for months by the UK team at Viper Books. Those in the know included Claire Beaumont, Hannah Westland, Georgina Difford, Angie Curzi, Drew Jerrison, Flora Willis, Rosie Parnham, Alia McKellar, Therese Keating, and Niamh Murray, who pulled out all the stops to make *The Christmas Appeal* something special.

The intriguingly festive cover was created by Steve Panton, while the text was proofed by Jane Howard and copyedited by Mandy Greenfield. The audiobook was created by Louisa Dunnigan and Audrey Kerr.

For this US edition I would like to thank my wonderful editor at Atria, Kaitlin Olson, and her unflappable editorial assistant

Ifeoma Anyoku. Huge thanks also to production editor Sonja Singleton and copy editor Lisa Nicholas, without whom you wouldn't be holding this book in your hands right now. Of course, it's thanks to the hard work of marketing specialist Maudee Genao and publicist Megan Rudloff that you heard about it in the first place. I am so lucky to have such a committed and creative team in the US.

My wonderful agents, Gaia Banks and Lucy Fawcett, at Sheil Land Associates have been the loveliest, most helpful, supportive, and industrious elves for this book, as for all my others. Meanwhile David Taylor is unswerving in his support. Thanks to Alba Arnaud for her expert handling of foreign rights and to Lauren Coleman for her assistance. Across the Atlantic, I am grateful to my US agents, Markus Hoffmann at Regal Hoffmann & Associates in New York and Will Watkins at ICM Partners in L.A.

In the course of this story, I refer to The Prison Optician Trust, a small registered UK charity that provides training in optical skills for former prisoners and helps them find paid work in the optical sector. More details can be found at www.prisonopticians.org.

Any story about The Fairway Players is inspired, at least in part, by my thirty years as a member of The Raglan Players in Northolt. The group staged my first-ever play, *It's My Manor* (cowritten with Sharon Exelby), in 2005 and my second, *Bump in the Night*, in 2009. Together they triggered the writing bug that led me down the long and winding path to this book. If you appeared in either of those plays or worked behind the scenes, I have a lot to thank you for.

Former Raglans who remain friends include Arnie Johnson, Jane Nicholls, Keith Baker, Felicity Cox, Terry & Rose Russell,

Liam Tebbit, Emma Green, Darrell Van Der Zyl, Vince Alderman, Jaqui & Neil Sampson, Rochelle Griffin, Richard Edwards, Mary Almeida, and Jan & Mick West. Also former Raglans, but much more besides, are my fellow witches: Sharon Exelby, Carol Livingstone, and Wendy Mulhall. Our coven nights casting spells around the cauldron are the best.

Meanwhile my oldest school friends, Samantha Thomson and Alison Horn, are perennial sources of energy, sense, and positivity.

This book is dedicated to the Ghost of Christmas Past, and I share the same shadowy sense of what might have been with the wonderful Ann Saffery, who came into my life an impossible fifty years ago and has never been far away.

Finally, in 1984 Gary Stringer walked into a Raglan Players audition and was cast in Alan Ayckbourn's *Confusions*. He played my long-suffering partner in that show, and I'm delighted to say he's never been out of character since.

## About the Author

Janice Hallett is a former magazine editor, award-winning journalist, and government communications writer. She wrote articles and speeches for, among others, the Cabinet Office, Home Office, and Department for International Development. Her enthusiasm for travel has taken her around the world several times, from Madagascar to the Galapagos, Guatemala to Zimbabwe, Japan, Russia, and South Korea. A playwright and screenwriter, she penned the feminist Shakespearean stage comedy *NetherBard* and cowrote the feature film *Retreat*. She lives in London and is the author of *The Appeal*, *The Christmas Appeal*, and *The Twyford Code*.